What the critics say about
BROTHERS BELOW ZERO

"This is a solid read that blends family dynamics
and intense action in its exciting, satisfying climax."
—*School Library Journal*

"Seidler captures the bonds that can exist between
the young and the elderly. He also has a keen
appreciation for the small details that make up life."
—ALA *Booklist*

"Seidler takes on an age-old story line—jealousy
and competition between two dissimilar brothers—
and spins it into a survival story with a soft mystical
edge."

—*Kirkus Reviews*

TOR SEIDLER

BROTHERS BELOW ZERO

ILLUSTRATIONS BY PETER McCARTY

LAURA GERINGER BOOKS

≜ HARPERTROPHY®
AN IMPRINT OF HARPERCOLLINS PUBLISHERS

Harper Trophy® is a registered trademark of HarperCollins Publishers Inc.

Brothers Below Zero
Text copyright © 2002 by Tor Seidler
Illustrations copyright © 2002 by Peter McCarty
For information address HarperCollins Children's Books, a division of HarperCollins
Publishers, 1350 Avenue of the Americas, New York, New York 10019.

Library of Congress Cataloging-in-Publication Data
Seidler, Tor.
    Brothers below zero / Tor Seidler ; illustrations by Peter McCarty
        p.   cm.
    Summary: Having lived for years in the shadow of his younger, more talented brother,
middle schooler Tim takes painting lessons from his beloved Great-aunt Winifred and
discovers that he is a gifted artist.
    ISBN 0-06-029179-6 —ISBN 0-06-029180-X (lib. bdg.) — ISBN 0-06-440936-8 (pbk.)
    [1. Brothers—Fiction.   2. Great-aunts—Fiction.   3. Death—Fiction.   4. Artists—Fiction.
5. Self-esteem—Fiction.   6. Vermont—Fiction.]   I. McCarty, Peter, ill.   II. Title.
PZ7.S45526 Br   2002   2001024019
[Fic]—dc21   CIP
                                                                                AC

Typography by Alicia Mikles
❖
First Harper Trophy edition, 2003
Visit us on the World Wide Web!
www.harperchildrens.com

For John Morron Seidler

R. TUTTLE took a break halfway through his pork chop. It was awfully tough.

"Glad to be out of the salt mines for a few days, boys?" he asked, setting his fork down.

"Yeah," said John Henry.

Tim just nodded, afraid his father was about to bring up first term report cards. It was the Friday before Christmas.

"What did you do all day, sing carols?" Dr. Tuttle asked.

"We sang 'Jingle Bells' in assembly," Tim said.

"We had a scrimmage this afternoon," John Henry said. "Last one of the season. It was cool."

"It must have been," said Mrs. Tuttle. "The high for the day was ten degrees."

"Aw, you don't notice that when you're playing, Mom. Do you, Timmy?"

Tim grunted. His fingers had been numb the whole scrimmage, but it hadn't really mattered, since he'd never gotten near the ball—even though John Henry had thrown over and over to the boy he was meant to be covering. "Trying to make your kid brother look good?" the coach had said when he finally took Tim out. Tim was in seventh grade at Burlington Middle School, John Henry in sixth.

"Me and Spider . . . I mean, Spider and I connected for four TDs," John Henry said. "Should have been five. The last one hit him right in the breadbasket and he dropped it—didn't he, Timmy?"

Tim mumbled unintelligibly, his mouth being full of roll.

"You missed it? Yeah, I guess you were on your butt." John Henry grinned at his mother. "Spider faked him out of his shorts."

"Shorts, on a day like this?" she said. "That seems awfully spartan."

"It's just an expression, Mom. It means he made Tim look like a dork."

The rolls were on the stale side, but Tim had lubricated his with enough butter to get it down. "The field was icy," he muttered. "And my glasses fogged up."

Luckily, ice reminded Mrs. Tuttle of a pipe that had burst that morning in the storage room of the Burlington Art Museum, where she volunteered as a tour guide.

"*Ethan Allen and the Green Mountain Boys* got soaked," she said.

"How ignominious," said Dr. Tuttle. "They outfox the British army for the whole Revolutionary War, only to be laid low by a burst pipe."

"I imagine they'll survive," Mrs. Tuttle said. "They're in bronze."

"Ah, a sculpture. I was thinking you meant the painting."

"No such luck. *That's* up in the main gallery. Every time I have to call it 'a masterpiece of American historical painting,' the words stick in my throat."

"Is it as bad as one of Aunt Winnie's *View*s?" John Henry asked, smirking.

"Aunt Winnie's paintings are beautiful!" Tim cried.

"It's not a fair comparison," said Mrs. Tuttle. "Winifred doesn't pretend to be a real painter."

"But she *is* a real painter," Tim said.

"I'm very fond of her *View*s," said Dr. Tuttle.

For Christmas and his birthday Dr. Tuttle always received one of his aunt's small oil paintings of the view of the Green Mountains from her house. Winifred wasn't his real aunt, only his aunt by marriage. Long ago, during World War II, she'd married his uncle, but soon afterward his uncle had been shot down in the Pacific, leaving her a widow. Mrs. Tuttle considered her paintings "amateurish," so Dr. Tuttle always took them to hang in his lab at the university.

"Don't you like the chop, Trev?" Mrs. Tuttle asked.

"Very flavorful," Dr. Tuttle said, preparing for a second assault.

But John Henry rescued him by slipping an envelope from his back pocket and sliding it toward him.

Tim felt the opposite of rescued as he watched his father set down his knife and fork and pull out John Henry's report card.

"Uh-oh," Dr. Tuttle said.

"What is it, dear?" said Mrs. Tuttle.

"Somebody we know got an A minus in arithmetic." He spoke gravely. "What do you suppose could have happened?"

"I missed a quiz the week you took us to Baltimore for your conference!" John Henry cried. "It still counts as straight As, doesn't it?"

"Of course it does, lambie," Mrs. Tuttle said. "Your father's just pulling your leg. Where's yours, Tim?"

"You always say bringing reading material to the dinner table isn't polite," Tim said.

"Report cards are an exception, dear."

"I dropped it on the bus and somebody stepped on it. I think it got smudged."

"Well, we'll do our best to decipher it."

"To tell you the truth, Mom, I'm not sure where I left it."

"I think you went straight up to your room when

we got home," John Henry said helpfully.

"Shall I come up and help you look?" Mrs. Tuttle offered.

"Um . . . no, that's okay," Tim said, pushing his chair back slowly from the dinner table.

He trudged upstairs to his room and groped under his mattress, where he'd stashed his report card in hopes that one of his great-aunt Winifred's sayings— "Out of sight, out of mind"—would hold true. In his opinion it was a nasty trick to hand out report cards right before Christmas, which was supposed to be the season of joy and glad tidings and ho, ho, hos.

He walked back downstairs in slow motion, hoping his peas might at least get cold enough for him to use that as an excuse for not eating them.

"Let's see it, sweetie," Mrs. Tuttle said as he shuffled into the dining room.

He was nearer his father's end of the table, however, and handed the report card to him. Dr. Tuttle was in charge of a team of scientists who did genetic research at the University of Vermont Medical Center. He believed that grades were the result of genes.

Unfortunately, he soon passed the report card on to Mrs. Tuttle, who believed grades had more to do with studying.

"Really, Tim," she said with a sigh. "If you spent half as much time on your homework as you do eating Winifred's chocolate-chip cookies, you wouldn't have all these Cs."

"Or that gut," John Henry murmured, loud enough for only Tim to hear.

"Now, Alison," Dr. Tuttle said gently, trying to get down another bite of leathery pork. He'd actually been wishing Mrs. Tuttle spent *her* time in a different way, though he would never have dared say so. When she wasn't volunteering at the art museum, she was putting in time at the Women's Shelter or working for the local chapter of the Campaign for Women's Rights. "Aunt Winnie's a good old soul," he said. "I'm sure she's not a bad influence."

"She's fat and weird," John Henry said.

"She is *not*," Tim said.

"Living up on that hill all by herself. She's so out of touch, she's—"

"Now, John Henry," said Mrs. Tuttle, "it's not

nice to say mean things about poor old Winnie."

"She's not poor," Tim said.

"Don't you be touchy, dear. And don't forget your peas."

"But Mom, they got cold."

"Shall I heat them up for you?"

Tim shook his head with a sigh. In fact, peas were just as bad hot as cold. "I finished my meat," he pointed out.

"But vegetables help you grow, dear. And they're good for your eyesight."

She didn't say "Look at John Henry." She didn't have to. John Henry, who didn't have to wear glasses, had cleaned every pea off his plate.

Tim was used to suffering in comparison with his brother, but that night it bothered him more than usual. He actually lay awake in bed brooding about how he was a year and two months older than John Henry and still worse at just about everything. But if nothing else, the miserable scrimmage had worn him out, so he didn't lie awake too long. And when he woke up, it was bright and sunny and—best of all—

Saturday. Saturdays were wonderful—particularly winter Saturdays. This time of year it got dark too early for visiting Great-aunt Winifred's hilltop after school, so he had to wait till Saturday to see her.

Saturday was Mrs. Tuttle's day at the Women's Shelter, and since Tim had slept kind of late, she was gone by the time he got down to the kitchen. But his father was still there, making rings on the front page of the paper with his coffee mug, and John Henry was poring over the sports section.

"I could take you boys Christmas shopping," Dr. Tuttle offered.

"I was thinking I'd hit the mall Monday," said John Henry. "I'm helping Mr. Cooley clean his milking machines today. He's giving me three bucks an hour."

"How magnanimous," said Dr. Tuttle. "What about you, Tim? Do you have something in mind for your mother yet?"

"Maybe I'll shop Monday, too," Tim said.

Dr. Tuttle didn't press the point. The truth was, he hated taking days off from the lab, even on weekends. Once he was gone, John Henry grabbed his parka and a pair of galoshes and took off. After a couple of extra pieces of toast smeared with raspberry jam, Tim donned his parka and hiking boots and set off as well.

Dr. and Mrs. Tuttle both worked in Burlington— Vermont's biggest city—and both Tim and John Henry went to Burlington Middle School, but they lived out in the country, three miles east of the city limits, next to the Cooleys' dairy farm. Their mailing address was Williston, which was just a village—"no bigger than a gnat's eye," according to Great-aunt Winifred. But Great-aunt Winifred didn't even live in Williston. Her hilltop was a couple of miles farther east, not in any village at all.

As Tim walked down the road past the Cooleys' farm, his eyes kept returning to their barn—not because John Henry was in there cleaning the milking machines but because of the way the steam was coiling out of the cupola. With all the cows inside, the barn got as hot as it did smelly, and in the sunlight the escaping steam was strangely beautiful, twisting across the glinting tin roof and spiraling up into the powder-blue sky.

After the Cooleys' house came Cooley's Curve, and a quarter mile past that, a dirt road merged into the main road on the right, marked by a solitary mailbox with W. V. TUTTLE stenciled on the side. Tim opened it and pulled out a bill from the electric company and a copy of the *Burlington Free Press* and headed up the dirt road. Cut through pines and hemlocks, it was shady and noticeably colder than the main road, but Tim felt warmer with every step. He snapped mental photos as he climbed: of a squirrel who hadn't hibernated yet, his showy tail the same ruddy gray as a dawn sky; of a four-point buck who managed to look graceful even while gnawing bark off a tree trunk; of a slinky creature that darted under a fallen log before Tim could tell if it was a mink or a weasel. He paid less attention to the noises—a chainsaw wailing in the distance, crows cawing irrita bly in the creaky old trees—till he rounded the last switchback and heard a tinkling sound.

He passed a big clump of yew and walked around his great-aunt's garage—an old two-tone Chevy was pulled up to it—and headed for the house. It was white clapboard with shutters the exact same dark green as the yew and wisps of smoke slipping out of the fieldstone chimney. The tinkling came from an assortment of wind chimes hanging from the eaves of the front porch, but Tim walked around to the back door. As soon as he stepped into the mudroom, he smelled something scrumptious. Molasses cookies, he was pretty sure. He shut the door softly behind him, dumped his parka and gloves and hat and scarf on the woodpile, kicked off his boots, opened the inner door, and stepped into the glorious warmth of the kitchen. Definitely molasses cookies, he thought, sniffing at the wood stove.

He propped the mail against the rolling pin on the counter and padded through the dining room and front hall to the threshold of the living room. Great-aunt Winifred was sitting at her easel in the picture window with her back to him, her hair a fuzzy white aureole in the slanting-in sunlight. Poor old Ben Franklin wasn't around anymore—he'd made it to twelve, which was eighty-four in dog years—so Tim could easily have crept up and surprised her. But he didn't. Great-aunt Winifred was eighty-four in people years, an age when sudden shocks might be dangerous.

Tim bristled whenever John Henry called Great-aunt Winifred fat, but in fact she *was* a bit over-weight. It took her a couple of seconds to swivel around in her paint-speckled Windsor chair when he cleared his throat. Her glasses were thicker than his, with gold rims instead of black, but even as the sun glinted off the lenses, half blinding her, a smile lit up her round face.

"Timmy!" she said, blinking at him.

"Hope it's okay I didn't call first."

She laughed at this absurdity. He walked across the faded Persian carpet onto the drop cloth and gave her a hug.

"Lands, child, you're cold as a codfish!"

She set her brush on the edge of her palette—it was on a candle stand by her easel—and pulled a handkerchief from the sleeve of her dress to wipe his drippy nose. After rocking back in her chair, she heaved herself to her feet.

"Hot cocoa or hot cider?" she asked. "The cider Jeb brought's as fresh as tomorrow morning."

Jeb Grimsley, the grocer's son, delivered her gro-ceries in his Jeep once or twice a week.

Tim picked cider, and while she went after it, he pulled a chair up beside hers and studied her painting. It had progressed since last Sunday. Now you could tell that the snowy summit of Mt. Mansfield, which poked up over the treetops out the window, was shaped like a man's profile. She never seemed to get it quite right—this time the nose on her mountain was considerably more bulbous than the nose on the real one—but he couldn't have cared less.

She brought him a mug of steaming cider with a stick of cinnamon in it and sat back down. Once, last winter, he'd used the cinnamon stick as a straw and scalded his tongue, so he pushed it aside and blew on the surface before taking a birdlike sip.

"Mm, good." He set the mug on the windowsill. "Your painting's good, too. Almost done."

"It better be—it's your folks' Christmas present. Are they okay? Trev sounded a little squirrelly when he called on Wednesday."

"He had a cold he couldn't shake."

"I can imagine. He's wise as a treeful of owls—but he doesn't have enough sense to stay home when he's sick."

"He hates not going into the lab."

"And how's your mother? Running around to beat the band, I suppose." Great-aunt Winifred laughed fondly. "That woman's busier than a long-tailed cat in a room full of rockers! She called me from that funny thingamajig last week, but I couldn't understand a word she said."

"Her cell phone."

"That's something I'll never understand. As if telephones aren't bothersome enough at home—now people want to carry them around in their pockets! And how's John Henry?"

Tim sighed.

"What's the matter, dear heart?"

"Nothing."

"He's not sick, is he?"

"Nope. He got straight As again."

Great-aunt Winifred chuckled, which made her whole body jiggle. "He's sharp as my aunt Tilly's sewing shears, that boy."

"Yeah."

She gave him a close look. Her eyes, slightly magnified by her glasses, were the same faded blue as the sky over Mt. Mansfield. "You don't seem quite yourself today, child. What's the matter?"

"Oh, I got mostly Cs again. And I stink at football." He found himself leaning to the left, so that his head fell against her soft shoulder. It smelled like molasses cookies. "I'm more than a year older than he is, Aunt Winnie, but he's an inch taller."

"John Henry?"

"Yeah. And he can shinny to the top of our flagpole in ten seconds flat. I can't even get halfway up. And if we race home from the bus, he's at the front door before I'm at the mailbox."

"Mm, he's quick as a rabbit downwind of a fox."

"Yeah, and he can toss the football right over the Cooleys' barn. A perfect spiral. I can't even get it to the roof. And when we play Space Invaders in the video arcade on Church Street, he wins every time. Same with Minesweeper."

"Minesweeper?"

"On the computer. He's even better at shoveling snow than me. And mowing the lawn."

"He's something, all right. But what difference does it make to you?"

"Just . . . he's better at everything."

The Windsor chair squeaked as Great-aunt Winifred pivoted around and put an arm around Tim's shoulders. "You two may be as different as chalk and cheese but think how boring it would be if you were just alike. And you're the sweetest boy I know."

"I am not. And even if I was, that's not being better at something."

"Land o' Goshen, child. Don't you know how silly it is to compare yourself to others? It's useless as two tails on a dog."

"But when people see me and John Henry, they always feel sorry for me. I can tell."

"So what? People feel sorry for me, too. They look at their neighbors, and look at me, and they say, 'Poor old thing, living up there all by herself.' But does it do them any good? Or me any harm? I may be a poor old thing, but I'm a happy one." She kissed the top of Tim's head. "And you know what makes me happiest in the whole world?"

"What?"

"Seeing you."

The warmth of the house had been bringing the blood back to the surface of Tim's skin, making his cheeks tingle, but now the tingling spread through his whole body, chasing out all the depressed feelings he'd had since dinner last night. When his great-aunt rocked backward to get ready to stand up, he clutched her arm, keeping her in her chair.

"What is it, Timmy?" she said, laughing.

"I like you here."

"Well, I like being here. But if I don't get to the stove in the next minute and a half, the cookies I've got in the oven'll be black as a tinker's pot."

Tim pondered this for a few moments and then let her go.

2

ON THE RARE OCCASIONS that Great-aunt Winifred ventured down from her hilltop, she never exceeded fifteen miles per hour in her vintage Chevy, and the only drivers who didn't mutter under their breaths when they got stuck behind her were farmers on their tractors. These rare occasions included the visits she paid the Tuttles on birthdays and, weather permitting, Christmas.

That Christmas, weather permitted. A few inches of snow fell on the twenty-third, but by the twenty-fifth even the road up her hill had been plowed.

Great-aunt Winifred, not being much of a shopper, always brought homemade gifts. Dr. and Mrs.

Tuttle got her latest version of *The View*. John Henry, who was turning into a daredevil snowboarder, got a hand-knitted ski sweater. Tim's present was the smallest: just an envelope. It contained a hand-painted card with a miniature version of her latest *View* on the front. Inside, in her cramped handwriting, was the following message:

> *Dearest Timmy,*
> *You always seem to like watching me at my easel, so this year I thought I'd offer you painting lessons (if you want them).*
> *All my love, GAW*

If he wanted them! He jumped up and hugged her so hard, her laugh turned into a gasp. While watching her paint, he often felt his fingers itch for a brush. "I'd use a little dark blue there," he would say to himself, or "I'd stick in a cloud over that birch tree."

Great-aunt Winifred's latest painting of the view ended up, as usual, in Dr. Tuttle's lab. As for the ski sweater, John Henry chalked up points with his mother by donating it to the Women's Shelter. The sweater featured splotches of pink and purple, and he wouldn't have been caught dead in it. But Tim's present was a success. He only wished it wasn't winter, so he could have a painting lesson every day! But at least there were the weekends.

For the first few lessons, Great-aunt Winifred had Tim make pencil sketches. They sat at her kitchen table, which was covered with a checkered oilcloth, and she guided him through a drawing of a plate of fresh-baked ginger snaps. It took three sessions. By the end of the first, the cookies were stone cold, but he added the steam rising off them from memory. His next project was the wood stove, which he drew with the oven door open and a spice cake inside. Then he drew the old gingerbread man who leaned in the window over the sink. Tim stuck in a blackbird hovering outside, hungry for a bite.

After the lessons they had hot cocoa in the living room, and Tim's eyes always wandered to the paint box on the candle stand by the easel in the picture window. Finally, on a Saturday in February, Great-aunt Winifred decided he was ready to try her paints.

She preferred good old-fashioned oils herself, but she also had fast-drying acrylics, and Tim took to these. He set up a makeshift easel right beside hers so they could both work on *The View*. His first attempt took six weekends.

"Why, it's quite good," Great-aunt Winifred declared when it was done. "It really is, Timmy—though the clouds are a little odd. I never saw clouds with green in them."

"Everything's so black and white in the winter," Tim explained.

"And you wanted some color. Of course. I never thought of that. It adds atmosphere, doesn't it?" Her eyes sparkled behind the thick lenses of her spectacles. "You know, I think sticking in the windowpanes is a wonderful touch. At first I thought it was a mistake—probably because I never thought of it myself. They make it look so cozy, don't they? Just like us. We're snug as two bugs in rug, aren't we, dear heart? I couldn't be happier if I were twins!"

Tim laughed, leaning against the plump old lady.

"Now all we need is something to celebrate your first real painting," she said. "I made a batch of peanut brittle last night. Would it be gilding the lily if I made a carrot cake to go with it?"

"No! I'll bring in some more wood for the stove."

Tim wasn't getting any skinnier, and when the sap started to rise in the maples and the robins started returning from the south, his parents encouraged him to join John Henry's Little League team. John Henry wasn't so sure this was a good idea. Needless to say, he was a much better fielder and batter and base runner than Tim—in fact, he'd finished second in the Most Valuable Player vote last year, and this year hoped to win. But although it was always fun to outshine his older brother, Tim was so crummy at baseball that John Henry feared the team might turn against him just for being related. Besides, you couldn't help feeling a little bit sorry for the poor klutz. So when Tim argued that he would get plenty of exercise walking up to Great-aunt Winifred's house every day after school, now that the snow had melted and the days were longer, John Henry sided with him. He also pointed out that if Tim joined the team, he would probably just end up sitting on the bench eating peanuts. So Dr. and Mrs. Tuttle finally conceded the point.

Tim started painting every day. He didn't lose any weight, thanks to Great-aunt Winifred's baking, but he worked hard on his *Spring View*, keeping in mind all her advice. He completed his second painting just before school let out for summer, and his progress impressed Great-aunt Winifred so much that she secretly ordered him an easel and a box of acrylics from Pandora's Paints in Burlington.

Two weeks later she was waiting for Tim out on her front porch when Jeb Grimsley's Jeep pulled up next to her Chevy. Jeb carried her groceries up to the porch. He'd also picked up her mail for her, which included a box from Pandora's Paints.

"Why, Jeb," she said, "you look dry as a thistle. Did you bring any cider?"

"We was fresh out, Mrs. Tuttle. But I stuck in a half gallon of lemonade."

"Then let me give you a glass."

Jeb, who was twenty-five years old, would have preferred a beer, but he sat on the porch glider and downed a glass of the lemonade. He didn't refuse a second glass, nor did he refuse to sample a piece of the cherry pie that was cooling on the porch railing.

He and Great-aunt Winifred were just finishing their slices of pie—Jeb was actually on his second—when Tim shuffled up with his hands buried in his pockets and his eyes on the ground.

"Hey, Tim," said Jeb. "Didn't see you on the road."

"I came through the woods," Tim muttered, climbing the porch steps. "Hey, Aunt Winnie."

"Why, Timmy, you look like the undertaker who lost his last casket," said Great-aunt Winifred. "What's the matter?"

"We got final report cards yesterday. Mom thinks I should go to summer school."

A piece of cherry pie had a cheering effect on him, however. And though it was strange to get a present when it wasn't his birthday and he'd ended up with mostly Cs again, the easel and paint box lifted his spirits even more.

Best of all, his father soon managed to convince his mother that his grades weren't quite bad enough to warrant summer school. So he didn't have to give up his vacation. He spent a great deal of it sitting at his new easel on Great-aunt Winifred's front porch. Their easels were separated by only a small wicker table, usually with a pitcher of lemonade and a plate of freshly baked cookies or lemon squares on it, but now they kept the easels angled away from each other so they wouldn't be influenced by each other's work. And when they quit for the day, they put their canvases in different rooms to dry. Tim worked even harder on his *Summer View* than he had on his *Spring View*—though it wasn't really work, as far as he was concerned. The only thing he loved more than dabbing paint on the canvas was listening to his great-aunt. His mother said she talked your ear off because she lived alone, but it didn't matter to him if she was talking about painting ("I'm just a Sunday painter, Timmy—real painters are scarcer than feathers on a frog") or the weather ("The wind was blowing so hard this morning, I'll bet Mr. Cooley's hens laid the same eggs four times"), there was nothing he loved more than the comfortable sound of her voice, with the wind chimes tinkling in the background.

Great-aunt Winifred was determined to finish

her summer painting by Dr. Tuttle's birthday, which was August twenty-fifth, and on the afternoon of the twenty-first she set down her brush and announced that she was done. Tim set his brush down just five minutes later.

"Both finished at once!" she exclaimed. "And started together too! What do you say we lean them on the porch railing and size them up?"

"But you always say comparing's silly—like me and John Henry."

"Not to compare, dear heart—not to see which is better. I just meant, for fun and profit. I'll give you some pointers—and maybe you can give me some back!"

So they propped their paintings up side by side. Great-aunt Winifred looked at them with her glasses on, then with her glasses off, then with her glasses on again. For once, she didn't have a single word to say.

3

WHILE TIM WAS PAINTING, John Henry wasn't always playing baseball. He also did odd jobs for Mr. Cooley. Some of these jobs weren't a lot of fun—like shoveling manure out of the cow barn or cleaning the chicken coop. But Mr. Cooley paid a fair wage, and by the middle of August, John Henry had saved up nearly a hundred dollars.

At dinner a couple of nights before Dr. Tuttle's birthday, John Henry came up with the novel idea of buying his father's present with his own money.

"That way it'll mean something," he said.

Tim, who hadn't earned a penny all summer and secretly spent his allowance on sweets, nearly choked on a mouthful of dry chicken.

"I couldn't let you waste your hard-earned money on me, John Henry," Dr. Tuttle said, to Tim's immense relief. "But you know what would be terrific? If you boys would help me put in that split-rail fence along the back of the property. You know how long I've been talking about it."

John Henry wasn't too disappointed. He figured he was bound to be a better fence builder than Tim. "The Cooleys have a couple of posthole diggers we can borrow," he said. "You get us everything else, Dad, and we'll do the work. Right, Tim?"

"Sure," said Tim.

The next day Dr. Tuttle bought the rails and the treated posts and staked the spots where the postholes had to be dug. On the morning of his birthday—it was a Saturday—John Henry got Tim up right after the Cooleys' rooster crowed so they would be able to finish the fence that day. As the two boys walked out across the backyard with the Cooleys' posthole diggers over their shoulders, their boots left dark footprints in the glistening dew, while the sun, just risen over the foothills, lit up the devil's paintbrush in the Cooleys' meadow like candles. Tim snapped a mental photograph for a future painting.

There were forty-one stakes along the back of the dewy lawn, which meant they had to dig forty-one holes, each two and a half feet deep, for forty-one posts. John Henry volunteered to dig twenty-one holes, leaving twenty for his older brother.

Great-aunt Winifred said that preparing one decent flower bed in Vermont's rocky soil was "worse than picking quills out of a dog's mouth," and local farmers were known to mutter that the only thing the land was good for was connecting New Hampshire to New York. But the hunks of schist and granite John Henry hit with his digger didn't faze him a bit. He was in top shape from his farm work and the calisthenics they did before baseball practice, and his hands were well callused from shoveling and pitchforking and batting. By the time Mrs. Tuttle called them in to breakfast, he'd dug seven neat holes. Tim, however, hadn't finished his fourth. His glasses kept steaming up, and his hands were already developing blisters.

Since it was Dr. Tuttle's birthday, Mrs. Tuttle had decided to do something unusual: make breakfast. By the time Tim and John Henry washed their hands and sat down at the kitchen table, their poached eggs on toast were ready and waiting. The eggs might have been cooked a bit too long—in fact, they were pretty much hard-boiled—but the boys had worked up such appetites, they ate them anyway.

"I guess I won't cook yours quite so long, Trev," Mrs. Tuttle said.

Dr. Tuttle's eggs ended up so runny, they seeped right into his toast and turned it to mush. He really needed a spoon, but it seemed a little rude to ask for one, and by the time one arrived with his coffee, the mush had hardened and turned cold.

At this point the boys were getting up to head back to work.

"Want some help out there, boys?" Dr. Tuttle asked.

"No way, Dad," said John Henry. "It's your birthday."

By noon John Henry had dug fifteen holes. Tim was stuck on his seventh. This seventh hole kept ending up on a slant, thanks to an insidiously long root sent out by the sugar maple in the middle of their backyard. If only the tree had sent out a long branch, instead, to shade him from the broiling midday sun!

Mrs. Tuttle had driven Dr. Tuttle in to Burlington to buy him a much-needed new blazer for his birthday, so the boys made their own sandwiches for lunch. Afterward, John Henry peeled off his shirt and put on some number-twelve sunscreen before heading back out, but Tim, self-conscious about his doughy gut, just put on a straw hat and some work gloves. His hands were killing him. But the gloves didn't help. In fact, they caught his sweat, and when one of his blisters popped, the salt in his perspiration made it sting like the dickens.

By three o'clock John Henry had dug all twenty-one of his holes. The rest was a cinch. He stuck in the posts, tramped dirt around the bases, and inserted the split rails. So by the time their parents pulled into the driveway, half the fence was perfectly completed.

Dr. and Mrs. Tuttle strolled over to where John Henry was enjoying a glass of iced tea in the shade of the maple.

"Looks splendid, dear," said Mrs. Tuttle.

"Stupendous," said Dr. Tuttle, clapping his younger son on the shoulder.

"It was a breeze," said John Henry. "Sharp blazer, Dad."

"See, Trev, I told you," said Mrs. Tuttle.

Dr. Tuttle, who felt comfortable only in a saggy white lab coat, gave a shrug. "So, Tim," he called out. "How's it going?"

Tim looked up from his half-dug fourteenth hole. His eyes were bloodshot—the constant trickle of sweat was making them burn worse than his blisters—but the steamed-over lenses of his glasses and the shadow cast by the brim of his hat kept his parents from seeing this.

"I've hit a lot of rocks," he said, gasping for breath. "And a killer root."

"You look a little overheated, sweetie," said Mrs. Tuttle. "Why don't you take your shirt off?"

"I don't want to get sunburned."

"The sun's low enough now—it shouldn't hurt you," said Dr. Tuttle.

"That's okay."

"What do you say I spell you, son?"

"Well . . ." said Tim, who was about ready to keel over.

"But it's your birthday!" John Henry cried as his father started to shed his new blazer. John Henry set down his glass and picked up his posthole digger. "I'll finish the fence."

"But you've done so much already, love," said Mrs. Tuttle.

"No sweat, Mom."

Tim didn't really like bowing out, but one of his blisters had turned bloody, and another five and a half holes were frankly beyond him. So he let John Henry take over and rested in the shade, feeling about the size of a field mouse that was nosing around a cowpat in the Cooleys' pasture. When a red-tailed hawk dropped out of the sky and carried the mouse off, Tim almost envied him.

But he felt better once all the holes were dug and he could help put in the posts and insert the rails. Just as they were finishing, Great-aunt Winifred's old Chevy crept up the driveway. It took her forever to get out of the car with two packages, but she finally did, whereupon she made her way slowly over to the boys.

"Hey, Aunt Winnie," said John Henry.

"Hi, John Henry," she said. "Why, Timmy, you look like the bottom of a birdcage."

Tim took off his glasses and wiped his face with his sleeve. "We've been working all day," he said. "Or, at least, John Henry has. I took a break. But I'm still pretty beat."

"You should have put a pebble under your tongue."

"Why?"

"That way you can work all day without getting tired and nothing can hurt you."

John Henry restrained himself from rolling his eyes at this silly old-wives' tale. "What do you think of the fence, Aunt Winnie?" he asked.

"Why, it's cute as a bug's ear," she said.

Now he did roll his eyes. *Cute as a bug's ear!* What a stupid, demeaning thing to call his fence!

But Tim smiled for the first time since he'd seen the morning dew. "It is kind of cute, isn't it?" he said. "What did you bring, Aunt Winnie?"

"Well, I made a dessert. And this other's a birth-day present for your father."

"Now I wonder what that could be," John Henry said, eyeing the painting-sized package.

But Tim's eyes were on the white box on top of it. "What did you bake?"

"A Black Forest cake."

This was Dr. Tuttle's very favorite dessert. His favorite meal was leg of lamb, and Mrs. Tuttle had stuck one of these in the oven. Once the boys washed up from their labors, the family sat down to dinner.

Dr. Tuttle had a bit of trouble carving the roast. Mrs. Tuttle might have left it in the oven just a few minutes too long. But at last everyone was served, and as soon as Dr. Tuttle sat down, Mrs. Tuttle proposed a toast to him.

"Thank you, Alison," he said. "But we really ought to toast the fence builders. Here's to you boys!"

"To John Henry, you mean," Tim murmured.

"And to Winifred, for coming down from her hilltop paradise to join us," Dr. Tuttle said. "And to Alison, for making this wonderful meal."

They all clinked glasses—wine glasses for the grown-ups, milk glasses for the boys—and drank.

"You haven't commented on my new blazer, Winnie," Dr. Tuttle said after getting down a mouthful of lamb.

"It's very snazzy, Trev."

John Henry couldn't suppress a giggle at the word "snazzy." Everyone looked at him, so he said he'd just thought of one of Mr. Cooley's jokes.

"Why don't you share it with us," Dr. Tuttle suggested.

"Um, let's see," John Henry said, thinking fast. "He asked me how many people were dead in the cemetery on Colchester Avenue, and I guessed three thousand, and he said, 'Nope, all of 'em.'"

Everybody laughed except Great-aunt Winifred, who just smiled. She didn't seem to be talking as much as usual. Or eating much, either.

"Don't you like the lamb, Winifred?" Mrs. Tuttle asked.

"Oh, no, it couldn't be better," Great-aunt Winifred assured her.

"Would you like a different piece?" said Mrs. Tuttle. "The end piece, maybe?"

"No, thank you, dear, I have a gracious plenty."

"Did Timmy tell you about John Henry's award?"

"My, yes—Most Valuable Player in the Little League." Great-aunt Winifred beamed. "Congratulations, John Henry."

"Thanks," said John Henry, smushing his last overcooked lima bean onto his fork. "I'll show you the trophy after dinner, if you want."

"Anyone for seconds?" Dr. Tuttle said doubtfully.

No one piped up.

"Don't forget your lima beans, Timmy," Mrs. Tuttle said. "They're better while they're still warm."

"But I thought birthdays were special occasions," said Tim, who could almost taste the Black Forest cake.

"How do you expect to grow without vegetables, dear?"

Though she didn't bring it up, Tim had now fallen nearly two inches behind his younger brother in height. But John Henry decided not to rub this in by asking for seconds on lima beans. The fence had been a very satisfying triumph—and the truth was, he hated lima beans as much as Tim did.

No one turned down seconds on the Black Forest

cake, not even Mrs. Tuttle. After dessert, she said she'd serve coffee in the living room, and everyone migrated there except John Henry, who headed upstairs to get his trophy. When he walked into the living room with it under his arm, he saw that his father was unwrapping Great-aunt Winifred's latest boring painting of her *View*.

"Well, dear, happy birthday," Great-aunt Winifred said. "What do you think?"

Dr. Tuttle turned the painting toward Mrs. Tuttle, the family expert on beauty. Mrs. Tuttle's eyes widened.

"Why—it's good!" she exclaimed.

Great-aunt Winifred laughed, bringing out the crinkly lines around her eyes and mouth. "You needn't sound quite so surprised, Alison."

Mrs. Tuttle colored. "No, I meant—"

"You know I'm only teasing. What about you, Trev, dear? Do you like it?"

"Very much indeed," said Dr. Tuttle. Even if he didn't have quite as much taste as his wife, he thought he could tell a pretty picture when he saw one. "It's so much . . . the style's so much more . . ."

"So much richer than usual," Mrs. Tuttle prompted him. "It really is, Winifred."

"That's exactly the word I used myself—richer. The colors just *sing*, don't they? Let the boys have a look. What do you think, boys? Don't the colors sing?"

Dr. Tuttle turned the painting so the boys could see it. John Henry didn't really look at it. He just thought it was weird for Great-aunt Winifred to get so excited about something—as if she had forgotten she was an old lady. Tim, whose face was already red from all the sun he'd gotten, turned even redder. Although it was now in a fancy frame, the painting was the *Summer View* he'd done himself.

"Really, Winnie, thanks a million," said Dr. Tuttle. "I think . . . sweetheart, what do you say we hang it over the fireplace?"

"Fine," said Mrs. Tuttle. "I'm tired of that still life anyway. Don't you think it would look nice there, Winifred?"

Great-aunt Winifred's plump body began to jiggle. She'd always been amused by the way her past presents disappeared into her nephew's lab. "A good place for it," she agreed. "Though you might ask Timmy what he thinks. He painted it."

Mrs. Tuttle had just picked up her demitasse, and a splash of coffee leaped out of the little cup onto her white summer blouse. But instead of rushing off to the kitchen to get out the stain, she just set the cup in its saucer and stared at Tim. Everyone stared at Tim.

"It's that beautiful frame," he said. "The frame does wonders for it."

But it was the painting, not the frame, that Dr. and Mrs. Tuttle couldn't get over.

"Here I've been grousing about you forgetting your chores," Dr. Tuttle said.

"For heaven's sake, Timmy, you might have *told* us you had artistic talent," Mrs. Tuttle said, sounding almost resentful. "I know we're only your parents, but still."

"Artistic talent?" Tim said, staggered. He'd never been talented before. "I only did what Aunt Winnie told me."

"And the pupil leaves the teacher in the dust!" Great-aunt Winifred said gleefully. "I've half a mind to throw my brushes away."

Dr. Tuttle took the still life down from over the mantelpiece and hung Tim's *Summer View* on the hook. Mrs. Tuttle declared that it was made to go there.

"You must have paint in your blood, Timmy," she said proudly.

Tim looked down curiously at the dried blood caked on the broken blister on his left hand.

"He's a natural, all right—a born artist," said Great-aunt Winifred. "Now, is this that trophy of yours, John Henry? My goodness, what a thing! But you have to remind me—is Little League football or basketball?"

"Baseball," John Henry muttered.

"Of course, baseball—the summer pastime— peanuts and Cracker Jacks. How marvelous!"

4

JOHN HENRY didn't think anything was very marvelous just then. In fact the painting over the fireplace made him sick to his stomach. Now that he looked at it, even he could see that it was pretty good.

A week later John Henry overheard his mother talking to his grandmother long distance in Florida. "Mm, the boys are fine," Mrs. Tuttle was saying. "We went back-to-school shopping yesterday at the mall. . . . Yes, John Henry's still shooting up like a weed. But, Mother, listen—you're not going to believe your other grandson. He's becoming a real artist! We've hung one of his landscapes over the fireplace. I can just see it in a museum someday, with a plaque: 'The Early Work of Tim Tuttle.'"

To John Henry this was like finding a worm in his corn on the cob. How could Great-aunt Winifred, who barely knew baseball from football, have taught Tim so much so fast? If only *Summer View* would disappear!

But it wouldn't. All through September Mrs. Tuttle couldn't walk into the living room without pausing in front of Tim's painting and sighing with pleasure. Even Dr. Tuttle, who thought of the paintings in his lab as a sort of wallpaper, would smile over the top of his evening paper at *Summer View*. It was the most miserable month of John Henry's life. School started again, and he got an A on his first social-studies test, but when he broke the good news at dinner, his parents' smiles seemed fake compared to the ones they bestowed on Tim's painting. Worse, when Tim got a C on his first math quiz, Mrs. Tuttle said it was nothing to worry about.

"I know how hard you're working on your *Fall View*, love. The leaves are turning such splendid colors this year, too. You must be having a field day."

"It *is* fun," Tim admitted. "I never got to use orange before."

"Guess what I made for dessert. I'll give you a hint—it's your favorite."

"Apple crisp?" Tim said hopefully.

Mrs. Tuttle nodded, smiling. "Of course, I know mine won't hold a candle to Winifred's, but I thought I'd give it a whirl."

"How adventuresome," said Dr. Tuttle.

Tim, who had eaten a bowl of his great-aunt's apple crisp only the week before, knew after one bite that his mother was absolutely right. As a matter of fact, she'd left out the cinnamon altogether. But remembering what Great-aunt Winifred said about comparing things, he assured his mother that it was delicious.

The apple crisp made John Henry's teeth ache, and in bed that night he lay awake trying to come up with a way to sabotage *Fall View*. One idea was to sneak up to Great-aunt Winifred's house in the middle of the night and pour black paint all over Tim's canvas. But people would probably suspect him, and besides, Tim would just start a new one. He thought of beating Tim to a pulp. He knew he could do it. But Tim was such a wimp, he'd never give him any provocation.

Then there was the idea of breaking Tim's glasses. But Tim had an extra pair, and breaking both would arouse suspicion.

Schemes like these began popping into John Henry's head at odd hours of the day. For the first time in his life a teacher accused him of daydreaming in class. A few days later he was out on the football field doing jumping jacks with the rest of the team when he realized the coach's "Hey, brain-dead!" was aimed at him. He'd forgotten his helmet!

"I've got to get my mind off that darn *Fall View*," he muttered as he trotted back to the locker room.

5

But an hour later, when they got off the school bus, it made John Henry cringe to see Tim rush straight off toward Great-aunt Winifred's hilltop. It was a crisp, sunny day, the first of October, and with the leaves hitting their peak, the hill looked as if a rainbow had melted all over it. Tim's *Fall View* would probably be so gorgeous, their parents would want to fly it from the flagpole.

The days were shortening, and Tim hated to waste easel time on such a perfect afternoon, so after checking Great-aunt Winifred's mailbox—it was empty—he actually broke into a jog. But the first section of the dirt road was the steepest, and after a couple of hundred yards he had to plunk down on a mossy roadside stump to catch his breath. While he was resting there, a pair of ruffed grouse—Great-aunt Winifred called them "partridges"—paraded out from behind a fern. The beautiful birds were usually hard to spot, what with their camouflaging plumage, and these were the first he'd ever seen with winter leggings half grown in.

He didn't jog the rest of the way, but he walked at a good clip, eager to tell Great-aunt Winifred about his sighting. It was a still afternoon. Even up on the hilltop, which was usually blowy, there wasn't a breath of wind, so as he came around the final switchback, he didn't hear the tinkling of the wind chimes on the porch. And when he slipped in the back door and dumped his books on the woodpile, he didn't smell anything baking. He walked through the kitchen and dining room and front hall. On Labor Day they'd moved their easels inside, into the living room, but Great-aunt Winifred wasn't there.

"Aunt Winnie?"

She didn't answer. But he'd just walked past her Chevy, so she had to be home. He went back to the kitchen and opened the cellar door. It was dark, but he called down anyway. No reply. He went out onto the front porch. She wasn't rocking on the glider or out in the garden cutting the last chrysanthemums. Staring at the silent wind chimes, he could hear his heartbeat.

Though Great-aunt Winifred wasn't a napper, he clomped upstairs and knocked on her bedroom door. No answer. He tentatively opened the door. The curtains were drawn, and at first the room was so dim that all he made out were the bunches of white roses in the wallpaper. But as his eyes adjusted, he saw a lump in the old four-poster bed.

"Aunt Winnie? Are you sick?"

She didn't answer. He tiptoed up to her bedside.

"Aunt Winnie?"

Her eyes opened. But her glasses were on the night table, and after blinking at him blindly, her eyes closed again.

"Aunt Winnie! What's wrong?"

Again her eyes opened. So did her lips. But all that came out was a gurgling sound, like a baby.

There used to be only one phone in the house—down in the kitchen—but Dr. Tuttle had insisted on having one installed in her bedroom in case of emergency. Tim grabbed it and called the lab. One of his father's grad students picked up.

"I need to speak to Dr. Tuttle," Tim said in a hoarse voice.

"He's in the clean room," the student said importantly.

But Tim was so urgent that she went to get him, and after a minute Dr. Tuttle came on the line.

"What is it, Tim?"

"Something's the matter with Aunt Winnie! She can't talk!"

"Where is she?"

"In bed. She's— she's—"

"Slow down. Is she breathing all right?"

"She's breathing, but she's— Something horrible's wrong, Dad!"

"Try to keep calm, Tim. I'll be there as soon as I can."

Dr. Tuttle's lab was right next door to the Fletcher-Allen Hospital, and in less than twenty minutes he and two paramedics pulled up in front of Great-aunt Winifred's house in an ambulance. They found Tim standing by her bed, holding her hand. Dr. Tuttle opened the curtains and joined Tim at the bedside. By the look of his poor old aunt, he guessed that she'd suffered a coronary or a serious stroke.

"You'll have to move, Tim," he said sadly. "So they can get her on the gurney."

Tim wouldn't budge. Finally Dr. Tuttle had to pry the boy's hand from Winifred's and pull him aside.

While the paramedics shifted the old lady onto the gurney and rolled her out of the room, Tim stared out the window at the view.

"Don't you want to come along to the hospital?" Dr. Tuttle said, laying a hand on Tim's shoulder.

Tim shook his head.

"You're sure?"

Tim nodded.

"Don't give up hope, son."

Dr. Tuttle gave Tim a hug and hustled off after the paramedics.

6

"COME ON, LAMBIE," Mrs. Tuttle said from the doorway to Tim's bedroom. "It's after ten."

Tim responded by putting his pillow over his head.

"We've only got an hour, Tim. Surely you don't want to miss it—you of all people."

The pillow remained firmly in place. Mrs. Tuttle turned with a sigh and went back downstairs to the kitchen. Dr. Tuttle and John Henry were sitting at the table in their Sunday best, even though it was Saturday.

"He won't budge," Mrs. Tuttle said.

"He's scared of the graveyard," said John Henry,

looking up from the box scores. "He always hated it when kids sang that one about worms crawling all over your snout."

Mrs. Tuttle's nose wrinkled up as if a worm was crawling on *it*. "Will you try, Trev?"

"I don't see as you can make somebody go to a funeral, sweetheart."

"But there'll be so few people there as it is."

Dr. Tuttle trudged upstairs, not feeling very hopeful. He'd gotten Winifred to the hospital alive, but she'd died shortly thereafter. This hadn't been a big surprise to the paunchy on-call doctor in the emergency room. He'd already contacted Winifred's personal physician and learned that for the past year she'd had an inoperable heart-valve condition. She hadn't broadcast it because she hadn't wanted people making a fuss. When Dr. Tuttle tried to explain this to Tim later that night, the boy shrugged and walked out of the room as if the subject interested him no more than going to the hospital had. Mrs. Tuttle said Tim was adopting the "ostrich approach": sticking his head in a hole in the ground.

At the moment, Dr. Tuttle saw, Tim was sticking

his head under his pillow. But he didn't try to roust the boy out of bed. He just went up and laid a hand on his shoulder and said:

"Try not to feel too bad, son. We'll see you in a while."

Mrs. Tuttle was right about the crowd at the funeral. Living on her secluded hilltop, Great-aunt Winifred hadn't had a wide circle of friends, and there were only about a dozen people on hand in the Unitarian church in Burlington. The minister said some comforting words about how Winifred was surely smiling down on them from heaven, but not many looked as if they put much stock in this—least of all Dr. Tuttle, who firmly believed that people live on after death only in the genes they pass down to their children. This made him all the sadder, since his aunt had been childless. He decided then and there to leave her paintings of *The View* up on the walls of his lab.

Small as the group at the funeral was, every one of them, including Jeb, the grocer's son, and Pandora Potts, the owner of Pandora's Paints, followed the hearse to the cemetery on Colchester Avenue and watched with damp eyes as the casket was lowered into the earth. Even John Henry shed a few tears, thinking of the joke he'd made about the cemetery the last time he saw his great-aunt alive. Now that she was dead, he also felt a bit guilty about having always thought of her as weird and fat and old.

But Tim never shed a single tear over her. While the grave digger was shoveling earth onto her casket, Tim was sitting at the kitchen table munching on his second stale sugar donut in a row, studying a grainy photo of the wreckage of a plane crash on the front page of the paper. When his mother and father and brother pulled into the driveway, he was raking leaves in the backyard.

"You don't have to do any chores today, Tim," Dr. Tuttle said.

Tim shrugged and went right on raking as if it was a day like any other.

7

DR. TUTTLE had to go to the lab that afternoon—one of the experiments he was supervising was in its final stages—but instead of heading off to check on the Women's Shelter, as she wanted to do, Mrs. Tuttle spent as much of the rest of the day as possible with Tim. He seemed fine, but he never asked about the funeral, never spoke a word about Great-aunt Winifred. After the boys went to bed that night, Dr. and Mrs. Tuttle discussed Tim's situation. They agreed he must be going through a period of denial and decided not to bring up Great-aunt Winifred until he did himself.

The next day it poured, and Dr. Tuttle stayed home and organized a game of Monopoly with the boys. He did everything in his power to help Tim win, going so far as to trade him Park Place for Connecticut Avenue straight up, which outraged John Henry. But in the end John Henry bankrupted both of them anyway. Tim wasn't a sore loser, though. And he ate all his dinner, even the succotash.

On Sunday evenings the family usually watched TV together. That night there was a comic movie on about identical twins who were separated at birth and found each other as adults. Mrs. Tuttle privately thought it was juvenile, but Dr. Tuttle, who'd done several genetic studies of identical twins, was enjoying it as much as the boys—at least until a commercial for homeowners' insurance came on and John Henry said:

"What's happening with Aunt Winnie's house, anyhow?"

Dr. Tuttle took a sip of his decaf and cleared his throat. "Well, I guess she left it to me. Come spring, maybe we can have it fixed up."

"To sell?"

"That's a bridge we don't have to cross till the will's out of probate."

"What's 'probate'?"

"Where are you going, love?" Mrs. Tuttle said, watching Tim head out of the living room.

"I'm kind of tired," he said.

"But the movie's not over!"

Tim just shrugged and inched toward the door.

"You know, son," Dr. Tuttle said, "you can still use Winnie's house. You can go up anytime you want and paint the view."

The next morning Dr. Tuttle gave Tim a key to Great-aunt Winifred's house, but Tim stuck it away in his desk drawer. He had no more intention of going to her house than he'd had of going to her funeral. For if he hiked up there and found the house empty, it would be that much harder to keep on believing his great-aunt wasn't really dead. When the school bus lumbered by the cemetery on Colchester Avenue, a cold hand seemed to reach inside him and give his heart a warning squeeze, but otherwise all he had to do was close his eyes to see her perfectly, sitting at her easel or rolling out a pie crust. To him she was still vibrantly alive.

Nevertheless, he missed her dreadfully. Her old

saying—"out of sight, out of mind"—was a bunch of baloney. Finally, in desperation, he came up with an idea: painting a picture of her to hang over his desk. That way he would see her first thing when he came home from school, and if he woke up in the middle of the night feeling lonely for her, all he would have to do was turn on his lamp, and there she'd be.

Unfortunately, his easel and paint box were up at her house. But he saved up his allowances, and one Saturday he had his mother drop him off at Pandora's Paints on her way to the Women's Shelter. He bought four tubes of acrylics and a couple of brushes and a small canvas. In memory of his great-aunt, Pandora Potts threw in three more tubes of paint and three more canvases free of charge.

Later that day Tim rigged himself an easel out of scrap lumber from the shed and set it up in the sewing room, at the end of the upstairs hall—a room his mother hadn't set foot in in years. From then on he devoted all his spare time to his great-aunt's portrait, and though his parents didn't ask what he was painting, they were both pleased that he was doing it. He worked from memory and from a slightly yellowed snapshot of Great-aunt Winifred opening a Christmas present on their sofa. But after every session he ended up scraping his paint off the canvas, and as the days turned to weeks, he realized there was something in the joke his mother used to make about Great-aunt Winifred: that she stuck to landscapes because people were too hard to paint. People *were* hard. At least, Tim couldn't even come close to capturing his great-aunt.

One Saturday he heard a *thwunk*ing sound and, glancing out the sewing-room window, saw that John Henry was punting the football around one of the Cooleys' pastures. On the spur of the moment he decided to try painting a picture of his brother. The pasture, which sparkled with frost, came out very nicely—and so, to his surprise, did John Henry. Encouraged, Tim tackled Great-aunt Winifred again, starting from scratch. He worked painstakingly, every afternoon, right into December. But this attempt was even worse than his earlier ones. It was as if his brush refused to tell the truth. The portrait didn't even remind him of his great-aunt, and he missed her more than ever.

One of their family traditions was to hike partway up Great-aunt Winifred's hill to cut their own Christmas tree, but since Tim hadn't mentioned her once since the funeral, Dr. and Mrs. Tuttle put their heads together and decided it would be safer simply to buy a tree this year. While the family was decorating it, John Henry announced that he was making a change of his own this year. He was going to use his own money to buy his presents.

"I don't care what you say," he declared as he carefully hung his favorite ornament, a grapefruit-sized one coated with silver and gold sparkles.

"That's a very generous impulse, dear," said Mrs. Tuttle, wondering why that hideously gaudy thing was never one of the ornaments that broke. "But I'm not sure it's a good idea. What do you think, Trev?"

Dr. Tuttle looked up from his struggles to get their oldest strand of Christmas lights, which was "in series," to work.

"Sorry," he said. "This thing's more frustrating than isolating the DNA of a drosophila."

"John Henry wants to use his own money to buy his presents," Mrs. Tuttle said.

"But you worked so hard over the summer, J. H.," said Dr. Tuttle. "Wouldn't you rather spend your hard-earned cash on that new snowboard you've been carrying on about?"

"That's okay," said John Henry, who secretly hoped to get a new snowboard from them. "I'm too old to take present money from you."

"Well, if that's how you want it," said Dr. Tuttle. "But don't feel you have to march in step, Timmy."

This was small comfort to Tim. If his younger brother was too old to take present money, how could he possibly accept it?

After school that next Thursday the two boys got off the school bus at the mall on Route 2. John Henry's wallet was bulging with over a hundred dollars in cash. He bought their father a fishing reel for twenty-nine dollars and their mother a thirty-two-dollar scarf of green-and-yellow silk. Tim, however, couldn't find anything decent for five dollars and thirty-one cents—his current net worth—and he plodded home feeling guilty and disheartened.

Things went downhill from there. The next day first-term report cards were handed out, and Tim's was no better than last year's. Halfway through dinner that night John Henry casually produced his. While his marks were getting their usual raves, Tim stared at his cauliflower, praying for a miracle to make his parents forget that he must have gotten his report card, too.

It worked. After praising John Henry's grades, neither of his parents said a word about seeing his.

This surprised John Henry as much as it did Tim. It annoyed him, too, since Tim's lousy grades always made his seem that much better. He waited patiently, but the subject of report cards seemed to have been dropped. Finally, after finishing off the last smelly bite of cauliflower, he blurted out:

"Eighth graders got report cards today, too."

"Mm," said Mrs. Tuttle. "How'd you do this term, Tim, dear?"

"Not so good," Tim mumbled.

"Well, it was a tough fall for you," Dr. Tuttle said.

Mrs. Tuttle agreed. Tim waited for them to say more. But his father just finished off his biscuit, while all his mother said was "I'm afraid I oversalted the cauliflower a bit, dear, but do try and eat some of it."

Tim lit into his cauliflower as if he actually liked it. And when he looked up gratefully at his parents, he had a brainstorm.

During dessert—ice cream and store-bought sugar cookies—he studied their faces. At one point he stared at his father so hard, Dr. Tuttle asked if he had a crumb on his chin.

Tim had one canvas left, and after breakfast the next morning he went straight up to the sewing room and began a double portrait of his parents. Christmas vacation had begun, and for the next few days he concentrated on the painting. His parents, busy as ever, were usually out when he felt like checking something—the size of his father's ears, for example, or the exact color of his mother's eyes. But, luckily, the upstairs hallway was a gallery of family photos. And when his parents *were* home, he surreptitiously studied their faces. And little by little the faces in the painting became recognizable.

A funny thing happened. Ever since his father had pried his hand out of Great-aunt Winifred's, Tim had been trying to dodge a feeling of loneliness and despair. But now, sitting between the painting of his parents and the painting of his brother, which was propped against the old pedal-driven Singer sewing machine, he began to feel less lonely and less desperate. Of course, he *was* alone in the sewing room. No one ever set foot in there except him. But he didn't feel so alone.

He put the finishing touches on the double portrait on the morning of the twenty-fourth, as a few Christmasy snowflakes knocked gently on the sewing-room window. As he wrapped the painting in foil and tied a ribbon around it, he felt a whirring in his stomach, an expectant feeling he hadn't experienced since he was hurrying up the hill to work on his fall painting and tell Great-aunt Winifred about the partridges.

The snowfall grew thicker and thicker. By evening it was a fierce blizzard, and in the middle of Christmas Eve dinner their electricity went out. Dr. Tuttle tried to call the power company, but the phone was out, too. No one was terribly concerned, though. There were plenty of candles, and it was kind of fun, eating by candlelight with the howling wind piling snow against the windows.

After dinner Dr. Tuttle built a blazing fire in the fireplace—the furnace was dead as well—and Mrs. Tuttle went upstairs with a flashlight and dug out extra quilts for the beds in case the heat stayed off all night. Then they gathered around the hearth to sing Christmas carols and hang stockings underneath Tim's *Summer View*. After that they all deposited their presents under the tree, which looked a little forlorn unlit, and then Dr. Tuttle sent the boys up to bed with the spare flashlight.

"Leave it on the post at the top of banister, Tim," he said. "I'm going to try to keep the fire going, but if—"

"What about Santa?" said Tim. "He'll burn his feet."

"I'm pretty sure old St. Nick wears fireproof boots," Dr. Tuttle said.

"If you boys get *too* cold tonight," Mrs. Tuttle said, "you can always crawl in with each other."

"Yuck!" cried John Henry.

Tim echoed this sentiment. But up in the bathroom he held the flashlight while John Henry brushed his teeth, and John Henry returned the favor.

"You know, if Santa Claus actually existed, he'd have a sleigh wreck tonight, huh?" John Henry said as he set the flashlight on the post.

Eighth grader that he was, Tim still actually liked to believe Santa Claus did exist, so he just said, "Sleep tight, John Henry," and felt his way into his room. His computer could run awhile on battery, so he flicked it on and started playing Minesweeper, but soon his fingers got too cold and he flicked it off and crawled into bed. The weight of the second quilt made him feel nice and snug, but instead of falling right to sleep, he slipped into a fuzzy place halfway between sleep and waking. It was sort of like the unheated mudroom at the back of Great-aunt Winifred's house: not quite inside, not quite outside. And in fact he felt himself floating up to that very room. Peering into the kitchen, he saw that Great-aunt Winifred was safe and sound, her face lit from the warm glow of a wood stove that was giving off the heavenly smell of non-store-bought cookies. . . .

He woke up in the middle of the night, blinking at the ceiling light. The electricity had come back on. But the room was bitterly cold, and before he could work himself up to desert the warmth of the bed to dash over to flick off the switch, the light flickered back out.

He soon dozed off again, but his brother, who'd been awakened by his bedside lamp coming on, didn't fall back to sleep when the darkness returned. John Henry had been having a bad dream. In it Tim was balancing on the banister post like the flashlight while their parents stood below on the staircase madly applauding, as if Tim had done something stupendous. It started John Henry wondering what his brother could have possibly gotten them for Christmas for a lousy five dollars and thirty-one cents.

After a while his curiosity got the better of him and, cold as it was, he slipped out of bed. He groped around for his heavy winter bathrobe and fur-lined slippers and then felt his way out into the spookily dark upstairs hall. Once he located the flashlight, he flicked it on and crept down to the living room. Dr.

Tuttle must have come down at some point to stoke the fire, for it was blazing away behind the fire screen, but the stockings still hung limp and empty from the mantel. It was disappointing to see that none of the packages under the tree was big enough to be a snowboard—but that wasn't what John Henry had come down for. Kneeling, he shifted the flashlight beam from package to package till it hit one with a bell-shaped tag that said *For Mom & Dad, Merry Christmas, Timmy*. It was on a flat foil package. John Henry wedged the flashlight between his thighs and undid the red ribbon and carefully peeled back the pieces of Scotch tape. The feel of the package made him uneasy, and when he pulled the foil away and saw the beautiful double portrait, he felt queasier than he had last summer while cleaning out the Cooleys' chicken coop. He could just hear his parents carrying on about the painting, forgetting the fishing reel and the silk scarf entirely.

8

I N THE MORNING the phone and electricity were still out. But the sun was out, too, and Dr. Tuttle was convinced power would soon be restored. He and the boys bundled up and went out to shovel the walkway and the driveway under a storm-scoured sky. They couldn't look anywhere without squinting, the reflection of the sun off the new snow was so brilliant; and the air was so cold, their nostrils tingled.

After finishing the shoveling, they carried a few extra loads of firewood into the house. Then everyone gathered in front of the blazing fire and plundered their Christmas stockings. As usual Tim's and John Henry's stocking presents were mostly practical:

underwear, soap, four-packs of Ticonderoga pencils, Scotch tape, socks, rulers. And at the bottom was the usual box of maple-sugar candy.

They all got new mittens, too, and Mrs. Tuttle put hers on before venturing into the kitchen. Mittens might have seemed an unfair handicap to someone who wasn't a world-class cook in the first place, but then cooking was out of the question anyway, since the stove was electric. No poached eggs. She couldn't even make toast. Nor could she stick the turkey in the oven. But she did halve a couple of the grapefruits her parents had sent from Florida.

After Christmas breakfast she usually called her parents, but she'd been unable to recharge her cell phone, and the regular phone was still dead, so they headed straight for the tree. The family tradition was for Dr. Tuttle to hand out presents in order of age, starting with the youngest. John Henry's first present was a book bag from his mother—which, he was relieved to see, didn't have any women's rights slogans on it. Tim's first present was three large tubes of acrylic paint—indigo, tan, and forest green—from his father. Mrs. Tuttle's first present was the scarf from

John Henry. She put it around her neck and went to check herself in the hall mirror. The green-and-yellow silk made her look a bit sallow, but she gave John Henry a big kiss and said he had exquisite taste.

"And it means even more, love, knowing you spent your own money on it. What do you think, Trev?"

"Very silky-looking," said Dr. Tuttle, who was unwrapping his own present from John Henry. "Hey, get a load of this!" He started playing with the reel. "Those trout better watch out, if they know what's good for them. Thanks a million, son."

"I hope it fits your rod all right," John Henry said.

"I'm sure it will. Now if you could just arrange to melt the ice on Lake Champlain . . ."

In years past Great-aunt Winifred had been next to open. By shutting his eyes, Tim could see her happy smile as she asked him to help her get the ribbon off a package.

"You're up again, tiger," Dr. Tuttle said, handing John Henry another present.

In the second round, John Henry got a pair of rechargeable foot warmers from his parents. They were ingeniously designed, slender enough to slip into his snowboarding boots, and according to the package, they stayed warm for up to four hours. Next, Tim opened a Swiss Army knife from John Henry.

"Wow, scissors . . . a saw blade . . . everything," Tim said, admiring it. "This one'll be perfect for scraping paint off when I make a mistake. Thanks a lot, John Henry."

But John Henry hardly heard him. A pounding had started up in his ears as soon as his father picked up the flat package in aluminum foil.

"Here's one for both of us, sweetheart," Dr. Tuttle said, handing it to Mrs. Tuttle and moving behind her chair.

An even louder pounding started up in Tim's ears. What if they didn't like the portrait as much as he hoped? What if the fact that he'd painted it had clouded his judgment? As his mother undid the ribbon, he stopped breathing altogether.

She pulled away the foil—and scowled.

"Well, this is a fine how-do-you-do. Who are these people supposed to be?"

Tim thought she was joking, pretending she couldn't tell who the subjects were. But she didn't laugh and say, "Just kidding, Tim, it's absolutely marvelous." She just kept scowling.

"Why, it's you and Dad," Tim said. "Can't you tell?"

Dr. Tuttle looked at it and scowled, too. "Is this your idea of a joke, Timothy?"

Tim flinched. His father used "Timothy" only when he was in trouble. "A joke? No, it's . . . I know it didn't cost much, but I worked hard on it."

"I can see that," Mrs. Tuttle said, running a finger above her upper lip.

"This is what you call the Christmas spirit?" Dr. Tuttle said, touching his nose.

John Henry had to clench his teeth to keep himself from chortling. Tim, bewildered, joined his father behind his mother's chair. In the portrait his mother had a mustache. His father had three warts on his nose.

"But . . . but . . . but Mom!" Tim sputtered. "I didn't give you that mustache!"

"Who did, then?" Mrs. Tuttle asked, feeling above her upper lip again.

Tim looked at his brother, but John Henry had put on an expression of perfect innocence.

Dr. Tuttle was still touching his nose. "The only warts I ever had were on the bottoms of my feet," he said. "And that was years ago."

"But I didn't give you those!" Tim protested. "Cross my heart and hope to die."

"Imagine what poor Winifred would have said," Mrs. Tuttle said, sliding the painting under her chair, "if she knew this was how you were going to put her painting lessons to use."

Bringing in Great-aunt Winifred this way was more than Tim could bear. A sob welled up in his throat, and he raced upstairs.

Up till then John Henry had been pleased with himself for the work he'd done in the middle of the night. It hadn't been easy, adding the warts and mustache by the light of the flashlight, his fingers half frozen in the icy sewing room. But the sound of Tim's door slamming upstairs gave him a pang. Had he gone a little too far?

Mrs. Tuttle walked back to the hall mirror to inspect her upper lip again. "*Not* a very nice joke," she said.

"You know, though," Dr. Tuttle said thoughtfully, "it doesn't really seem like Tim."

"He couldn't be starting the I-hate-my-parents phase already, could he? He's still just in middle school."

"I don't know. He never mentions Winifred. Maybe it's a symptom of repressed anger over her death."

"But why would he blame us for that?" Mrs. Tuttle wondered, drifting back into the living room. "Do you have any idea what this could be about, John Henry?"

"Huh?" said John Henry, lifting his eyes from his foot warmers.

"Do you know what could have gotten into your brother?"

"Tim?" he said, as if he had several brothers to choose from. "Search me, Mom."

9

PSTAIRS, TIM WAS LYING facedown on his bed, trying to hold back the tears. That horrible portrait wasn't what he'd painted at all! He wouldn't have put a mustache on his mother and warts on his father—not for Cadwallader and all his goats, as Great-aunt Winifred used to say. There was only one possible explanation: John Henry had unwrapped the package in the middle of the night and touched the portrait up.

But why would his brother do anything so cruel? John Henry was good at everything. There was no reason for him to want to ruin the one thing Tim was good at. The only other possible culprit was a ghost or poltergeist. And Great-aunt Winifred said that if there were such things as ghosts or poltergeists, she would have known about them, living by herself in an old house on a lonely hilltop.

How could his parents have believed he would paint them that way? He'd sworn he hadn't—and if people loved you, they believed you. Especially on Christmas. Besides, if *he'd* painted warts and a mustache, they would at least have looked realistic, not ham-fisted and tacked on like the ones in his painting.

He decided to jump out the window and go visit someone who appreciated him. He got up and dug the key to Great-aunt Winifred's house out of his desk drawer. But as he slipped it into his pocket, the cold cemetery feeling crept through him. In the bright light of day it was hard not to admit to himself that to visit Great-aunt Winifred, he might have to go to Colchester Avenue, not the hilltop.

But even a cemetery would be better than a place where people didn't appreciate you.

His parka and boots and deerskin gloves were down in the pantry—he'd taken them off there after helping with the firewood—but he could do without those things. Even though he and his brother weren't supposed to hitch rides, he could get one in to Burlington. He put on an extra pair of wool socks and squeezed his feet into his shoes and put on two of the sweaters Great-aunt Winifred had knitted him and the mittens from his stocking. Then he opened his window, knocked the snow off the ledge, and swung his legs out. The snow down below looked soft as a cloud.

But it wasn't. Landing threw him forward, and his forehead smacked the frozen ground under the new snow. When he stood up, the sun seemed to be fractured into a hundred stars.

The road hadn't been plowed yet. Tim weaved dizzily along it, trying to stick to some tire tracks. After a few hundred yards something blocked the low sun. It was Great-aunt Winifred's hill. As he stared at it, he couldn't think why in the world he was heading for Burlington. He climbed a stone wall and cut across one of the Cooleys' pastures.

His toes turned numb as he slogged through the snow, but he hardly noticed. It felt as if a top was spinning in his brain. What a funny bump on his forehead! It made him feel very peculiar. But he knew everything would be fine once he got to Great-aunt Winifred's house, because wood stoves don't need electricity.

10

"**T**HINK I OUGHT TO go upstairs and talk to him?" Dr. Tuttle said. "It hardly seems right to open presents without him."

Mrs. Tuttle sighed. "What a Christmas. First I can't cook the turkey, and now this. I knew we should have volunteered at the Women's Shelter."

But just then the lights on the Christmas tree blinked on. And they didn't blink off again. The furnace rumbled in the basement, and soon the radiators started to hiss.

"Maybe we can have a Christmas dinner after all," Mrs. Tuttle said.

Dr. Tuttle asked John Henry to help him sort the remaining presents while Mrs. Tuttle returned to the kitchen. Though she didn't bother preheating the oven, just getting the turkey into it put her in a better mood, and she decided to go upstairs and talk Tim into rejoining them. Tim didn't answer the knock on his door. When she opened it, an icy blast greeted her.

A minute later Dr. Tuttle and John Henry were standing with her in Tim's window, staring down at the dent he'd made in the snow. John Henry was amazed.

"Tim's usually so chicken about jumping," he said. "He'd never even go off the Cooleys' hayloft."

"Where on earth could he have gone?" Mrs. Tuttle said.

"Not far, I hope," said Dr. Tuttle, closing the sash. "It must be close to zero out there."

When they found Tim's boots and parka in the pantry downstairs, they figured he couldn't have gone far. Mrs. Tuttle suggested he might be sulking in the shed, but Dr. Tuttle came back from the shed shaking his head. He decided to call the police to tell them to be on the lookout for a runaway boy, but although the electricity was back, the phone was still dead.

"Darn thing," he said, slamming it down.

"Let's go after him, Trev," said Mrs. Tuttle.

"Mm. We'll need the chains."

John Henry helped him put the chains on the tires, but Dr. Tuttle thought it best he not come along. "Someone should be home in case Tim shows up," he said. "If he does, tell him . . . tell him . . ."

"Tell him we're sorry," said Mrs. Tuttle.

Left on his own, John Henry made himself a cup of hot cocoa with two marshmallows floating in it and took it into the living room and turned on the TV. There was going to be a football game on later, but at the moment the selection was pretty pathetic. He paused awhile on a documentary about climbing Mount Everest, but the description of the dangerous windchill factors near the summit gave him an uncomfortably guilty feeling, so he flicked to a bowling tournament. The house was getting warmer by the moment, and in spite of the regular explosions of bowling pins, his eyelids began to droop. He'd lost a lot of sleep last night, thanks to his late-night painting session in the sewing room.

The ring of the phone woke him. The bowlers

had turned into figure skaters. He hit the mute button and picked up the receiver.

"John Henry?"

"Hey, Mom. The phone's back."

"Any sign of Tim?"

"Um, nope." Checking his watch, John Henry was surprised to see that he'd slept two and a half hours. "No luck?"

"We've been all over the place. We called the Cooleys and the McDougals. All the shops and restaurants are closed. We went by the road up to Aunt Winnie's in case he got it into his head to go up there, but there aren't any tracks. Now we're at the police station here in Williston."

"Maybe he went into Burlington to catch a movie," John Henry said—though he doubted Tim had the money for a ticket.

"It's Christmas Day. The movie theaters are closed till later. Any other ideas?"

"Well, there's that weirdo, J. J. Billingsly, from his homeroom. He calls him about math sometimes."

"Thanks."

"Ten-four, Mom."

After hanging up, John Henry fished the soggy marshmallows out of his cold cocoa and ate them. Noticing the corner of the foil-wrapped painting peeking out from under his mother's favorite chair, he felt an uncomfortable pinch of guilt and shifted his attention to the presents in his pile. Under what looked discouragingly like a book was a simple envelope with J. H. written on it in his mother's neat script. The envelope wasn't sealed. He pulled out a card with a scenic photo of Camel's Hump, a nearby mountain, on the front. Inside, his mother had written: *One new snowboard of your choice from Woods Sporting Goods—Love, Mom & Dad.*

"Yes!" he cried.

He stuffed the card back into the envelope and reinserted it in his present pile. The present underneath, he noticed, was flat, wrapped in a page from the *Free Press*, with a bell-shaped tag that said: *For my big-little brother, John Henry, Merry Christmas, Tim.* Curious, John Henry slit the Scotch tape and pulled back the newspaper.

There he was! He carried the painting over to the window. As he studied it by daylight, he felt a clawing in his throat, as if he'd swallowed a beetle and it was trying to climb out. The painting—of him punting a football—was really cool. It made him look like a sports hero.

In the foreground of the painting was the split-rail fence, and what looked like a parade of ants crawling along one of the rails was actually a line of tiny letters that spelled out: *This fence was built by John Henry Tuttle*.

11

JOHN HENRY had an impulse to grab the Swiss Army knife he'd given Tim and use the saw blade on the fingers that had painted the warts and mustache on Tim's portrait. Why had he done such a rotten thing to his brother—his one and only brother? It was a hard question to figure out the answer to. But as he squinted at the snowy landscape outside the window and pictured Tim tromping along without his parka and snow boots, he did figure out one thing. Finding his brother would be better than sawing off his fingers.

He turned off the oven—the turkey was getting awfully brown—and wrote his parents a note. Then he put on his own snow boots and parka and his wool cap and deerskin gloves.

The first place he went was the shed, in case Tim was hiding behind the woodpile or in the canoe up in the rafters. He wasn't. So John Henry set off down the road.

About a hundred yards before he reached the Cooleys' driveway, he spotted a trail of footprints zigzagging across one of their pastures—toward the foot of Great-aunt Winifred's hill. He climbed the snowy stone wall and followed the tracks. But the drifts of new snow made the going slow, and he soon veered off toward the Cooleys' barn. The cows were mooing like crazy. Christmas must have delayed their second milking. He slipped in the side door, into the pump room. This was by far the cleanest corner of the barn—it housed two shiny steel vats where the milk was stored till the truck came to pump it out— but even there the cow stench was so thick, you could smell it even when you held your breath. John Henry took down a pair of snowshoes hanging on the wall between a two-man saw and an old leather harness. The Cooleys wouldn't mind him borrowing them.

The snowshoes made slogging along a little easier, and the trail of footprints soon led him up into the

woods. The snow wasn't so deep there, the branches overhead having caught a lot of it—which was probably why Tim hadn't used the road. Tim's trail weaved back and forth, as if he'd gotten tired, but once John Henry reached the hilltop and rounded the garage, he saw that the tracks led up Great-aunt Winifred's front porch steps and finally stopped to catch his breath, knowing his brother must be safe. Spread out before him was the famous view. The sun was setting, blood red behind the snow-white hills, and as he took it in, he wondered for a moment how Tim would see it if he was sitting at his easel. Tim's paintings *were* pretty good. Would Tim see more than he did? In spite of how cold the sewing room had been last night, and in spite of the fact that he'd just been sticking on warts and a mustache, there had been a curiously pleasant feeling of power in applying the paint.

The wind chimes tinkled as a blast of wind swept over the hilltop. John Henry kicked off the snowshoes and climbed the front porch steps. The front door was unlocked, but when he stepped into the house, it was as cold as a tomb. He flicked a switch, and the dusty old crystal chandelier in the front hall came on.

"Timmy?" he yelled, seeing his breath.

No answer. He called up the front stairs. No answer. He went through the entire house, flicking on lights upstairs and down, finally even checking the basement. Down there he found a shelf of forgotten Mason jars containing Great-aunt Winifred's applesauce and blackberry preserves. But there was no sign of his brother.

Back up in the kitchen John Henry heard a scratching at the back door. He opened it and caught sight of a porcupine scuttling off under a holly bush, leaving a thin trail in the backyard snow. Parallel to it was a bigger trail, made by a person.

The guilty feeling clawed at John Henry's throat again. Tim would never be able to make it all the way home—and besides, it was getting darker by the minute. John Henry picked up the kitchen phone to call 911. There was no dial tone. Either the lines on the hillside were down or his father had had the phone disconnected.

Trying not to panic, John Henry ransacked the

kitchen drawers. But when he finally found a flashlight, the batteries in it were dead. Everything about the house seemed creepy and cold and dead.

John Henry pulled his gloves on and hustled out the front door. He put the snowshoes back on and clumped around to the back of the house. Tim's tracks led him into the woods. The trail zigzagged among the pines and spruces and birches like a drunkard's.

It wasn't even four o'clock, but the last daylight was already dying, and as it did, the temperature seemed to dip another ten degrees. In a way this was a help. A crust formed on top of the snow so that John Henry's snowshoes didn't break through at all, making it easier to walk. But the trail was leading down the far side of the hill, away from everything he knew. And it was getting so dark, he had to bend over to make out the tracks.

At last they led out of the woods into a big clearing. Visibility was a bit better there, for a sliver of moon had risen, but it was still hard to follow the trail—and the trail was more crooked than ever. In fact, it was completely crazy, doubling back on itself here, going in circles there, leading him back over places he'd just been a minute earlier.

Then he saw a dark heap in the snow up ahead.

"Timmy!" he cried, breaking into a clumsy run.

The heap was definitely his brother, curled up on top of the crust. His shoes and jeans were dark, his socks and ski sweater and a funny old knit hat of Great-aunt Winifred's all sugarcoated with snow. John Henry kicked off his snowshoes and sat down on the crust and put Tim's head in his lap. He pulled off his gloves and wiped the snow from Tim's face.

"Tim? Are you okay?"

When Tim opened his eyes in the moonlight, John Henry stopped feeling cold for a moment.

"Thank goodness!" he said. "But why'd you leave Aunt Winnie's?"

Although Tim's eyes were open, they seemed to be glazed over. "She's dead," he whispered.

"Course she's dead. She's been dead for three months. Hey, where'd you get this bump? It's big as a quail egg."

Tim's eyes closed.

"What's with you, man?" John Henry cried. "Listen, I've got to tell you something." John Henry shook Tim till his eyes reopened. "It was me put on those warts and stuff—late last night. I'm really, really sorry. I don't know what got into me. When I saw the painting you made of me, I wanted to croak."

Tim blinked once.

"Do you forgive me?" John Henry asked.

Tim said something, but too quietly to hear.

"Huh?" said John Henry, leaning closer. "You forgive me?"

"For ruining my painting?" Tim said. "Or for making Mom and Dad think that's how I see them?"

John Henry swallowed. "Both?" he suggested, his own voice dropping to a whisper.

Tim looked at him in a way that made John Henry wonder again if painters saw more than ordinary people when they looked at something. But Tim said nothing, and after a few moments his eyes closed again.

"Hey!" John Henry shook him once more. "Can you get up?"

The eyes reopened.

"Come on, we've got to get back to Aunt Winnie's. We can make a fire in the stove."

"She's dead," Tim mumbled.

"Yeah, she's dead. But you still got me. And Mom and Dad. Come on."

John Henry shook him some more, but this time the eyelids stayed shut. He brushed the snow off Tim's sweater, took off his own parka, and put it on his brother. But Tim still remained out.

"God," John Henry groaned. "How am I going to get you back up to the house if you keep dozing off on me?"

The funny thing was, though, that he was feeling kind of drowsy himself. It seemed crazy, considering his long nap—though the narrator of the Mount Everest special had said something about intense cold making you sleepy. And hadn't he said something about how you were supposed to fight it?

A gust of icy wind swept across the clearing and cut right through to his bones. All he had on now was three layers—T-shirt, shirt, sweater—and for a moment the chill made him feel all too wide-awake. Struggling to his feet, he put his hands in his brother's armpits and started dragging him up the hill. By the time they'd gone ten yards—one lousy first down—John Henry was gasping.

12

BEFORE LEAVING the Williston police station, Dr. Tuttle called the Billingslys. But all this accomplished was to interrupt their Christmas dinner. They'd neither seen nor heard from Tim.

The Williston police had alerted the Burlington police to be on the lookout for a boy of Tim's description, but even so Dr. and Mrs. Tuttle kept driving around. When the daylight began to fade, they swung by the house and found John Henry's note, held to the refrigerator by a mountain-shaped magnet advertising THERE'S ALWAYS SNOW AT STOWE!

Turned off the turkey.

Gone to look for Tim—J. H.

"Ye gads and little fishes!" Mrs. Tuttle cried. "Now they're both gone!"

Alarmed as she was, she wondered at herself for using one of Winifred's old-fashioned expressions, and as they set off in the car again, she glanced out across the Cooleys' pasture at Winifred's hill— and noticed a trail of footprints winding across the pasture.

"Trev, pull over!"

He did, and she jumped out of the car and clambered over the plowed snow onto the Cooleys' snow-covered stone wall. From there you could tell that there were two different sets of tracks. One veered off to the Cooleys' barn and then remerged with the other as snowshoe tracks.

Dr. Tuttle joined her on the stone wall. "I'll bet that's John Henry going after him," he said.

"They're heading up Winifred's hill."

They scrambled back into the car and drove past Cooley's Curve and turned up the hill road. But the car couldn't make it up the first steep incline. Dr. Tuttle backed up far enough to get a head of steam and tried again. Again the tires ended up spinning, even with chains. By the third try, he had to put on the headlights.

"I shouldn't have been so hard on his painting," Mrs. Tuttle said suddenly. "He probably just meant it in fun."

"I was just as bad," Dr. Tuttle murmured, wiping the fogged-over windshield with a gloved hand.

After a half dozen futile attempts, Mrs. Tuttle said, "What we need is a snowmobile."

"Cooley sold his. He never used it."

"Do the police have them?"

They drove back to the Williston police station as fast as the chains would allow. A new sergeant had come on duty for the evening shift, a young man with rosy cheeks and a mustache wispier than the one Mrs. Tuttle had in the double portrait. He was working on a delicious, crispy-skinned turkey drumstick his wife had sent with him, but he stopped eating to listen to the Tuttles.

"Up that big hill in this weather?" he said, nipping

a fleck of turkey off his mustache with his tongue. "Gosh, it's supposed to go down to five below tonight."

"We couldn't even get up with chains—and now it's dark," Mrs. Tuttle said, trying hard not to sound like a hysterical mother.

"Doesn't some eccentric old biddy live up there?"

Dr. Tuttle cleared his throat. "My aunt *lived* up there, but she died in early October."

"Oh, gosh, I'm sorry," the sergeant said, his face turning rosier. "I didn't mean—"

"That's all right. The thing is, I'm not sure they could make it all the way to the house with the snow so deep. And even then, the heat's not on."

"Do you have any snowmobiles, officer?" Mrs. Tuttle said. "That's the only way we'll get up there."

"I'm afraid not."

"Then I'll have to drive back and walk up," Dr. Tuttle said grimly. "Do you have a high-powered flashlight I can borrow?"

The young sergeant pressed a button on his intercom. "Jonesy, will you take the desk?" he said into it. "I doubt Captain LaGrange is going to check in tonight, but if he does, tell him I'm out on search and rescue."

"Roger," said a crackly voice.

The sergeant stood up from his desk. "Come on, folks," he said, casting a wistful glance at his drumstick.

13

TIM FIGURED HE WAS DEAD. But he wasn't sure, because he'd figured he was dead before, and when he'd opened his eyes, he'd seen John Henry's face instead of an angel's. That was a while ago, though. Now he couldn't seem to open his eyes at all. At least not completely. By making a huge effort, he managed to slit one eye for a second. But this didn't help. It looked as if he was lying on a dim white cloud. Heaven? Or was it snow?

He tried to decide if he was cold. It was hard to tell. He just felt numb—and very sleepy. So sleepy, he simply couldn't stay awake any longer. And why shouldn't he just sleep?

As he was about to doze off, he gasped.

Something had tightened around his ribcage, pressing the air out of his lungs. The grip loosened. He took a couple of regular breaths and started to doze off again. Then the grip retightened, and he gasped once more. Someone was pressed up against his back, hugging him. John Henry? He tried to speak his brother's name, but his lips seemed to be frozen together, and he didn't have the strength to unstick them.

But it couldn't be John Henry. Last night, when their father had suggested they crawl into bed together for warmth, John Henry had said, "Yuck!" He wouldn't be hugging him. Somebody was, though. An angel? That must be what happened when you died: Angels grabbed you and flew you away like the hawk he'd seen carrying off the field mouse. He only wished he'd been able to paint Great-aunt Winifred once before he died.

As he was spirited away, he heard a plopping sound. It sounded an awful lot like the wind knocking clumps of snow off the trees onto the ground, but he figured it must be angels dropping other dead people onto the cloud. Then the sound got louder, much louder. It sounded like axes, chopping, and he realized he might be in the grasp of a devil, not an angel, heading not to heaven but to the other place, where you got minced up into little pieces.

But no, it had to be an angel. For he was rising up into the air. No doubt about it: It was the exact same feeling as in the elevator in the hotel in Baltimore last year. He relaxed once and for all and drifted off, ready to be reunited with Great-aunt Winifred.

14

JOHN HENRY WOKE UP feeling so tingling and toasty, he figured he'd died and gone to the other place. But when he opened his eyes, his mother's face was hovering over him. She had on the same Christmasy-green sweater as when they'd opened their presents in front of the fire, but her hair was strangely out of place—in fact, messier than he'd ever seen it. She leaned down and gave him a kiss on the forehead.

"My brave, brave boy," she said.

As she sat back up, John Henry made out a TV set beyond her head. The TV seemed to be suspended from the ceiling. "Where are we?" he asked.

"We're in the hospital, love."

"It smells funny."

"Mm. Drink something. The doctor said you'd be thirsty."

She held a blue plastic glass to his lips. The sip hole in the lid protruded sort of like the nipple on a baby's bottle. Pushing himself back against the pillows, he took the glass himself and screwed the lid off. His fingers were bright red and prickled as if he'd gotten into the nettles behind the Cooleys' chicken coop—though, of course, the nettles were buried in snow this time of year.

He *was* pretty thirsty, so he drained most of the ginger ale, even though it was lukewarm and didn't have much fizz. After he set the glass down on the traylike bedside table, his mother took both his hands in hers.

"What a Christmas!" she said, shaking her head in wonder.

Off to his right was a steamed-over window with a radiator underneath it. To his left another bed, the head hidden by a partially drawn curtain. Someone was moving behind the curtain; a foot wrapped in gauze was poking out of the blanket at the bottom of the bed.

"Who's that?" he asked.

"The nurse is with Tim."

A large black woman with heart-shaped earrings stepped out from behind the curtain.

"You're back with us," she said, smiling.

"How's Tim?" John Henry asked.

"He's a little woozy still. I'm hooking him up to an I.V. to keep his fluids up."

"Can I see him?"

The nurse pulled the curtain back, revealing a standing rod with a plastic sack of clear liquid hanging from it and, beyond that, Tim's rosy face on a pillow. He appeared to be asleep.

"Is he going to be okay?" John Henry asked.

"It's looking good," said the nurse, turning back to hooking up the I.V.

"Thanks to you," Mrs. Tuttle murmured, squeezing John Henry's tingly hands on the white thermal blanket.

The rumpled blanket reminded John Henry of the tracked-up hillside where he'd found his brother. He remembered trying to drag him up the hill and realizing it was impossible and lying down in the snow and giving Tim bear hug after bear hug to keep them both from dozing off.

"How'd anyone find us, Mom? Weren't we way over on the far side of Aunt Winnie's hill?"

"It was the sergeant. I don't know how we'll ever be able to repay him."

"What sergeant?"

Though Mrs. Tuttle had spent most of the last couple of hours with the man, she realized she didn't know his name. She'd been in such a panic the whole time, she'd never bothered to ask. "A young policeman from Williston."

"That twerpy guy who's been trying to grow a mustache?"

"Well, I don't think I'd call him twerpy, but yes, he does seem to be working on a mustache."

"He told me to slow down on my bike last summer. *He* saved us?"

Mrs. Tuttle nodded.

"Did he use snowshoes?"

"No, he—"

"Hey, what happened to mine? They're Mr. Cooley's."

"I don't know, love."

It felt oddly nice having his mother hold his hands, but he pulled them away so he could lean over the railing. There were no showshoes in sight. But on the right side of the bed there were a couple of interesting buttons. He pushed one. The back of the bed rose up.

"Cool."

He pushed the other and the foot of the bed started to rise.

"Please, honey," Mrs. Tuttle said. "I've had enough levitating for one day."

"Enough what?"

"Going up. We just got out of the helicopter."

"*What!* You got to ride in a chopper?"

"So did you. That's how we found you."

"No way!"

Mrs. Tuttle nodded. "Thank God the sergeant had a license to fly the thing."

"I was in a chopper? Where'd it land?"

She pointed up. "There's a helipad on the roof of the hospital."

"No way!"

She nodded.

"How fast did we go?"

"I've no idea."

"Where'd you take off from?"

"The airport. The sergeant drove us there in his squad car."

"His squad car! Did he use the siren?"

"As a matter of fact he did."

John Henry smacked the blanket, making his hand tingle more than ever. He couldn't believe he'd missed a chopper, a squad car, *and* a siren.

"The runways were shut down on account of the snow," Mrs. Tuttle said. "But helicopters don't require runways, thank goodness."

"How big was it?"

"Not very big. Four bucket seats. And what a racket!"

"I can't believe I didn't wake up! Is it still up on the roof?"

"I certainly hope the sergeant hasn't taken off. I haven't had a chance to thank him properly. John Henry!"

He'd catapulted out of the bed. But as soon as he

was on his feet, he had to grab the bed rail to keep from falling down. His feet were totally numb. They were also in funny red socks. And he was in a pale-green gown with an open back.

"I can walk," he insisted.

But he let his mother maneuver him back into the bed. He felt pretty shaky, and he really didn't want to be seen in a dress.

Standing at the bedside, his mother combed the hair off his forehead with her fingers. "You can visit the helicopter another time, lambie. It's freezing cold up there."

"Where's Dad?"

"Waiting outside. They only let two people in the room at a time."

Deprived of the helicopter, John Henry leaned away from her and jabbed at the buttons on the other side of the bed till he was like a piece of ham in a sandwich.

"For heaven's sake."

She moved around to that side of the bed and took over the controls, lowering the foot of the bed. As she sat back down, the nurse turned around.

"He's all set," she said. "Would you like some hot chocolate, young man?"

"Yeah!" John Henry said.

"Yes, please," Mrs. Tuttle corrected him.

"Yes, please."

When the nurse left, he looked over at his sleeping brother again.

"Were we frozen solid when you found us?"

"Pretty much," Mrs. Tuttle said.

"What happened? Tell me everything, Mom. Start at the airport. You got into the chopper . . . ?"

"Once they cleared the snow off it. They used one of those blowers, like I'm always telling your father we should get for the leaves. I got in back, and he sat up front. The sergeant showed us how to strap ourselves in and went through his checklist and fired up the rotor. Before you know it, we were rising up into the sky like a giant dragonfly."

"Wow!"

"It was cold at first, but by the time we were flying up Winnie's hill, the cockpit was fairly warm. We followed the road. Your father operated the searchlight."

"A searchlight!" Yet another missed-out-on novelty.

"It's mounted outside, with a handle on the inside. You can switch between wide and narrow beam. But we couldn't find any sign of you. Not even tracks."

"I followed Timmy's tracks up through the woods."

"Well, we landed in Winnie's backyard. And we were incredibly relieved when we saw your footprints going in the front. But the house was empty, and no one had stoked the wood stove. And there were no footprints going out. How could that be?"

"I saw Tim's tracks heading out the back. So I went that way."

"Huh. I guess the rotor blew the tracks away when we landed."

Mrs. Tuttle was looking at the window. Though it was steamed over, you could make out the snow piled up on the window ledge.

"Are you cold, Mom? You're shivering."

"It's just— It's all coming back to me. It was only an hour ago, but it seems . . . It was all such a nightmare, finding the house empty. We had no clue where you were. Trev said you'd probably gone back down to our house, but it was so cold out . . . We were desperate."

"You went back up in the chopper?"

"Mm. We zigzagged back down the hill toward Williston. One clearing we flew over was all criss-crossed with tracks, and there were two dark shapes in the middle. But when your father switched the searchlight to narrow beam, they flashed their white rumps and ran off."

"Deer."

But it was the black bear they'd spotted in another clearing that had sent her into a tailspin. Bears were supposed to hibernate, but there was no mistaking the creature who looked up irritably at the light source in the sky and lumbered off into the woods. Of course it was possible the boys had made it home—possible they were picking crispy skin off the turkey. But in her heart she'd been sure they hadn't been able to make it all the way back down the hill in that weather. Huddled in the backseat of the helicop-ter, she started to sob. From above they couldn't even distinguish animal tracks from human tracks! The jiggling contraption was so noisy, they couldn't hear her up front. She reproached herself again for being hard on Tim about the painting, and for being so caught up in her causes that she hadn't spent as much time as she should have with her boys. And now they were lost on the frozen hillside!

The search seemed more and more hopeless, but the sergeant was willing to keep at it as long as their fuel supply held out. In a last-ditch effort they were flying out over the far side of the hill when Mrs. Tuttle peered out the window and gasped. She blinked the tears out of her eyes and looked again.

"Trev!" she screamed, grabbing his shoulder. "Down there!"

Dr. Tuttle directed the searchlight's wide beam onto the clearing below.

"Jeez," said the sergeant. "I don't think deer did *that*, or a bear either."

The clearing was covered with tracks, tracks that formed the outline of a face—the face of a cheerful old woman who looked remarkably like Winifred.

"Give me a break," John Henry said when his

mother described this to him.

"I know it sounds crazy, but there it was." Mrs. Tuttle's eyes misted up again at the thought of it. "You two were curled up together right in the corner of her mouth."

"You're making that up."

"No, I'm not."

"Can we check it out in the chopper tomorrow?"

"I'm afraid landing and taking off wiped out most of it. But it was there. You boys must have tramped it out with your boots by sheer chance."

"Uh-uh."

"But how else could it have gotten there?"

"It wasn't me, Mom. I had on snowshoes. They didn't break the crust."

"Was it really Aunt Winnie?"

They both looked around abruptly. Tim, his head turned on his pillow, was looking at them intently.

"Timmy!" cried Mrs. Tuttle, moving over to his bedside. "How are you feeling?"

There was a purplish lump on his forehead, so to gauge his temperature she pressed the back of her hand against the side of his flushed neck. He felt warm but not burning up.

"Was it really Aunt Winnie?" he repeated.

"Yes, it really was," she said. "There was no mistaking it."

Tim gave her a long look. Then he turned his head and looked at John Henry. Then he looked back at her, nodded slightly, and closed his eyes.

15

"TIM WOKE UP," Mrs. Tuttle said when the nurse returned with a mug. "But now he's dozed back off."

"He's exhausted," the nurse said. "But it's a good sign. Here you go, young man."

"Thanks," John Henry said, taking the mug.

The nurse went over to Tim's bed and checked his pulse.

"He's getting his strength back," she said.

The hot chocolate didn't have any marshmallows in it, but it was warm and sweet. "Want some hot chocolate, Tim?" John Henry asked.

Tim made a sound that was halfway between a sigh and a moan. Then the door cracked open.

"The sergeant has to go, Alison."

It was Dr. Tuttle's voice.

"You go on, ma'am. I'll stay with them," the nurse said.

As Mrs. Tuttle stood up from Tim's bed, John Henry set the mug by the plastic glass and jumped down out of his own bed.

"Stay put, sweetie," Mrs. Tuttle said.

The soles of his feet still felt strangely tender, but John Henry could tell he wouldn't have any problem walking now. He grabbed a bathrobe off a hook on the bathroom door and put it on and followed his mother out into a corridor that had an even stronger smell than the room—sort of like the custodian's closet at school. His father was standing with the Williston policeman and a paunchy physician whose coat was the same pale green as John Henry's hospital gown.

"Who do we have here?" Dr. Tuttle said with a grin. He gave John Henry a hug. "How are you feeling?"

His father's hair was even messier than his mother's—but that wasn't so strange, since he often came home from the lab with his hair every which way.

"I'm okay," John Henry said.

"They couldn't keep *you* down for long, could they?" the doctor said, ruffling John Henry's hair. The round, black end of a stethoscope was poking out the side pocket of his coat.

"Tim woke up," Mrs. Tuttle said. "That's a good sign, isn't it?"

"Very," said the doctor. "There's that minor frostbite on the big toe of his left foot. But we caught it in time. Basically he's right as rain."

"Or sound as snow," Dr. Tuttle mused.

"I was so afraid he had hypothermia," Mrs. Tuttle said.

"He probably would have, if he hadn't had that parka on," the doctor said. "And it probably didn't hurt him to have a little extra layer of protection." He patted his paunch. "I always say, dieting's not all it's cracked up to be. I'll bet you're a great cook, Mrs. Tuttle."

"Well, I'm not sure I'd say *great*. But I do have a turkey in the oven. I don't suppose Tim will be able to come home for Christmas dinner?"

"He'd better stay with us tonight. There's that nasty bump on the forehead. We want to keep him under observation in case of concussion."

"What about John Henry?"

"I don't see why he can't go home with you."

"Speaking of that parka, J. H.," said Dr. Tuttle, "how'd it end up on Tim? When we found you in the snow, we got you two mixed up."

"You gave it to him, didn't you?" Mrs. Tuttle said, taking John Henry's hand.

"You're a hero," said the policeman.

John Henry grinned but felt a bit uncomfortable, his conscience prickling like his feet.

"So are you, officer," Mrs. Tuttle said, only now noticing the name tag on his uniform jacket. "John Henry, Sergeant Stankowski is the man who rescued you."

"Thanks a lot for saving my life, Officer."

"You're welcome. But it was your folks as much as me."

"They can't drive a chopper. I'm so bummed I slept through it!"

"Well, maybe I could take you up another time."

"Promise?"

"Really, sweetie," Mrs. Tuttle said. "You don't exact promises from people who've just saved your life."

"When the weather warms up, we'll go for a spin," the sergeant said with a smile. He turned to Mrs. Tuttle. "I better get going, ma'am. I'm sure glad everything turned out for the best. For a while up there I didn't think there was much chance of finding them."

Mrs. Tuttle seemed about to say something, but instead she stepped up and kissed the sergeant on the cheek, bringing a blush to his face. John Henry shook his hand, thanking him again, then followed his mother back into the hospital room. The nurse was sitting in a chair by Tim's bed.

"Sleeping like a baby," she said.

"Good," said Mrs. Tuttle. "The doctor says we can take John Henry home."

The nurse stood up. "I'll get you his clothes. We stuck them in a dryer."

As the nurse left, John Henry joined his mother at the foot of Tim's bed. "Think he'll be able to walk okay?" he asked, lightly poking the bandaged foot.

"I think so." Mrs. Tuttle pulled John Henry to her. "I can't get over how you went after him that way. If you hadn't found him and given him your parka . . . It's too horrible to think about. And it would have been all my fault. I can't imagine why I was so hard on that painting."

John Henry cleared his throat. "Um, I'm not so sure of that, Mom."

"Well, your father was kind of hard on him, too. Neither one of us would have been able to forgive ourselves."

"Um, I mean, I'm not so sure it was either one of your faults."

"What do you mean?"

While John Henry was telling his mother about his middle-of-the-night painting session, Dr. Tuttle was accompanying the sergeant up in the elevator that accessed the emergency helipad. It was cold as ever up on the roof, but at least there was no wind, and no antiseptic hospital smell. The man in the fluorescent-orange coveralls who'd guided them down earlier with light wands was nowhere to be seen, and the helicopter, its rotor listing to one side, looked rather forlorn, like a bird with a broken wing. Still, Dr. Tuttle had an impulse to run up and kiss it.

Of course his lips would have stuck to it if he had, so he contented himself with opening the pilot-side door for the sergeant. "This is going to sound pretty feeble, Sergeant Stankowski," he said, keeping the door open after the sergeant climbed on board. "But all I can do is second John Henry. Thank you for saving my sons' lives."

"It wasn't me, sir, it was that picture in the snow. Darnedest thing I ever saw. Looked just like an old lady, didn't it?"

"It certainly did."

"Maybe it was Mrs. Santa Claus—a Christmas miracle."

"Maybe. But if you hadn't been able to take us up in this thing, we'd never have found them."

"Well, as they say, your tax dollars at work."

"I'll never complain about taxes again." Dr. Tuttle gave the sergeant a heartfelt handshake. "Merry Christmas. You'll be hearing from us."

"Merry Christmas."

The helipad had a built-in heating element, so it

was pretty much free of snow, but even so the helicopter's liftoff created a bit of a flurry. Dr. Tuttle zipped up his parka and covered his face. Once the helicopter was well up in the air, he lowered his hands and stood watching its red taillight recede. The sergeant buzzed right over the building where Dr. Tuttle conducted his genetic research. When the helicopter disappeared beyond the toothlike crenelations of the lab building's roof, so did the *putt-putt* of the rotor. It was replaced in his head by an echo of the sergeant's words:

"It wasn't me . . . it was that picture in the snow. . . . Maybe it was Mrs. Santa Claus."

Dr. Tuttle knew very well who it had really been. Just as he knew who was responsible for Tim's "extra layer of protection." And as he stared off at the bite the lab building was taking out of the starry night sky, he felt a strange doubt in his lifelong belief in genes. Maybe it was just the subzero temperature making him lightheaded, or the fact that he'd eaten only half a grapefruit all day long. But—for a moment, at least— he wasn't so positive after all that passing down genes was the only way people could live on after death.

16

ON NEW YEAR'S EVE there was another blizzard, and the next morning a puffy quilt of new snow lay over Williston and the surrounding countryside. Dr. and Mrs Tuttle slept in, but John Henry got up early, determined to take care of his share of the snow shoveling before the kickoff of the first bowl game.

When he opened his bedroom curtains, he was nearly blinded by the sunlight bouncing off the fresh snow. But as his eyes adjusted to the brightness, he made out something red, just visible over the top of the roadside snowdrift, moving off toward the Cooleys'. He hooded his eyes and squinted. It looked suspiciously like that funny knit hat of Great-aunt Winifred's.

John Henry slipped down the hall in his pjs and opened the door to Tim's room. Tim had been kind of out of it all week, recuperating in bed from his Christmas adventure—but this morning his bed was empty. John Henry checked the bathroom and the sewing room. Nobody. He got dressed and hustled downstairs. Tim wasn't down there either.

From the back door John Henry saw a telltale path of footprints in the new snow. He was sure Tim shouldn't be exposing himself to winter weather again this soon, so he bundled himself up—parka, scarf, hat, mittens, boots—and followed the tracks out to the road. He soon wished he had sunglasses or his dark-lensed snowboarding goggles. Every single thing except the deep-blue sky was brilliant white, even the road. Though the snowplow had come by, it hadn't cleared all the way down to the pavement, and there'd been too little traffic to discolor the snow base. Even the TUTTLE on the side of their mailbox was whited out.

It wasn't easy to run in his boots, but he clumped along toward the Cooleys', casting sidelong glances at their snowy pastures as he went. No tracks at all.

At the end of Cooley's Curve he slowed up. Moving along the roadside ahead of him was an unmistakable figure. Tim's height, Tim's two-tone parka, Great-aunt Winifred's hat. Not quite Tim's walk—the boy was favoring his left foot—but that was on account of the frostbite on his big toe.

Fearing Tim was about to head up the road to the hilltop, John Henry decided he'd better stop him. The funny-colored big toe was supposed to get better, but it stood to reason that tromping through deep snow would make it worse. However, Tim passed up the hill road. And when he came to Route 2, he turned toward Burlington.

John Henry followed, leaving about half a football field between them. He didn't like to risk missing the first kickoff, but he was too curious to turn back. Nothing in the mall would be open this early. In fact, since it was New Year's Day, nothing would be open later, either.

But Tim passed up the mall.

Route 2 usually had quite a bit of traffic, but this early on a post-blizzard New Year's morning it was almost car-free. Even as they crossed over the freeway into Burlington, everything remained snow-muffled and peaceful. Now and then John Henry's boots squeaked on the packed snow, but Tim either didn't hear or was lost in thought, for he never looked over his shoulder.

Tim turned in at the first righthand entrance to the University of Vermont campus and headed straight for their father's lab building. But when he reached it, he passed it by. Had he decided he needed to return to the hospital? John Henry wondered. But Tim passed by the hospital, too. Had his concussion come back, making him what Mr. Cooley called "touched in the head"?

But when Tim turned right on Colchester Avenue, John Henry realized he knew where he was going.

The iron gates to the cemetery were open, and the path between the snow-laden pines had been plowed. When Tim came out of the pines' shadows at the top of the rise, he peered left and right, then headed in among the graves. John Henry hustled after him. The snow between the gravestones was deep, and there was no way in the world Tim would be able to locate Great-aunt Winifred's among the thousands of others.

"Hey, Timmy!"

Tim turned around, his cheeks chilled to match Great-aunt Winifred's hat. "John Henry. What are you doing?"

"Freezing my butt off."

"You followed me?"

"Yeah."

"How come?"

"I don't know. I guess I was afraid you might try to go back up the hill. You shouldn't be hiking around in this deep snow. My toes are getting numb already."

"Mine are fine."

"That's bad. It means there's no feeling left."

"No, they're toasty. I borrowed your new foot warmers."

"Oh."

"I didn't know you'd be coming out."

But it was fine with John Henry. He'd been thinking he'd have to carry Tim to the hospital on his back or something.

"You still shouldn't be out here. Mom'll have a cow."

"I woke up this morning feeling ten times better."

Tim turned and surveyed the interior of the cemetery: countless aisles of snowcapped gravestones interspersed with snow-clumped shrubs. After a moment John Henry walked past him, saying, "Follow me." He led Tim into the northeast sector, thinking he remembered the location of Great-aunt Winifred's gravestone from the day of the burial. Like most of the others, however, hers was a modest-sized slab of Vermont marble, and he ended up leading Tim on a winding wild-goose chase. Everything was so darn white!

But eventually he came to a tall, fancy monument with a pair of kneeling angels on top that he remembered from the burial. He'd thought how he wouldn't mind one like that for himself, but afterward his mother had rolled her eyes at it and made a comment to his father about bad taste.

Now that he was oriented, John Henry walked over to a nearby gravestone and swiped the snow off the front. It was an old slate one, so weathered the inscription was illegible. But the one next to it was newly cut marble.

"Here it is."

The polished stone bore the simple inscription:

WINIFRED V. TUTTLE

1915–2000

As Tim stepped up to the tombstone, John Henry backed away to give him some privacy. There was no wind at all; the only sound was the gurgling whisper of the falls in the Winooski River, beyond the border of the cemetery. If it didn't warm up a bit pretty soon, John Henry thought, even the falls would freeze.

Tim stood as still and silent as one of the stone angels, and John Henry felt a weird impulse to go up and put an arm around him. Of course he didn't. It was one thing to hug your brother for warmth when you were freezing to death on a hillside, another when you were right in the middle of Burlington.

"You okay, Tim?"

Tim couldn't speak. The stone with the engraved

name reminded him too much of the mailbox at the foot of the hill, conjuring up all the times he'd emptied the box and hustled up the windy dirt road.

"You okay?" John Henry repeated, hearing Tim sniffle.

If Tim replied, John Henry couldn't hear it. Then he watched him do something strange. Tim stepped up to the gravestone and knocked the snow off the top and tugged off a deerskin glove and pulled something out of his parka pocket and set it on top of the stone marker.

Moving up beside him, John Henry saw that it was a small rock.

"Is that from her garden or something?"

Tim shook his head.

"I know! It's what she said about if you keep a pebble under your tongue, you can work all day and nothing can hurt you."

Tim looked around in surprise, his reddened face glistening with quick-frozen tears.

"She said that the day we built the fence," John Henry said.

"Yeah," Tim said, putting his glove back on. "It's

too late to help her now, but still . . ."

"You never know. When you think about it, a gravestone's kind of like a tongue sticking out of the ground."

Tim tilted his head to one side, eyeing the gravestone. For some reason the idea cheered him up.

"Hey," said John Henry. "Why don't you paint a picture of her to remember her by?"

"Uh-uh."

"Why not?"

"I tried. Twice. After she . . . after she died. They came out awful."

"Third time's the charm."

"I doubt it."

"But it was," John Henry said.

"Huh?"

"That picture in the snow. You drew the whole thing—with your feet."

"I figure Aunt Winnie must have been helping me."

"Yeah, right. You did it. The way I see it, it's probably like hitting Coach's curve ball. If you can do it once, you can do it again."

Tim wiped the back of a glove across his face He wished he could have seen that picture in the snow before it got wrecked by the helicopter. But then, it had existed long enough to save them—and nothing, the gravestone seemed to whisper, lasted forever. Maybe that was enough.

John Henry was staring off in the direction of Great-aunt Winifred's hill and the Green Mountains. "You know, on Christmas there was the most amazing sunset up there," he said. "The sky looked like blood dripping down on the foothills."

"I sort of remember," Tim said. "It was beautiful, huh?"

"Yeah."

There was a silence—and Tim's eyes dropped to the ground. Silences had been rare with Great-aunt Winifred, but when there was one, she would say it meant someone was walking over your grave. And here he was, standing on hers.

He missed her so much, he wished he were down there with her. But then, if he were, who would there be to remember how wonderful she'd been?

"You know," he said, "I never really thanked you."

"For what?" John Henry said.

"Saving me on Christmas."

"Oh, well, after how I ruined your painting, what else could I do?"

"You could have left me there and gone back to the wood stove."

"Yeah, right," John Henry said scornfully.

"You know, I think I woke up in the helicopter. I thought someone was carrying me up to heaven."

"You *remember* the chopper?"

"Just for a second or two."

It took John Henry a while to swallow his jealousy, but he managed.

"You know, I was wondering something," he said.

"What?"

"I didn't want to bother you while you were sick in bed, but . . . do you remember when we were up there?"

"In the helicopter?"

"On the hill. In the snow."

"Most of it's kind of fuzzy."

"But . . . do you remember when I asked you something?"

"What?"

"If you'd forgive me for what I did to your painting?"

Tim snorted. "What do you think, Mr. Straight As?"

John Henry frowned, his hackles going up. But Tim smiled and said:

"Of course I forgive you. You saved my life."

"Oh. Well, I don't know about that." John Henry looked back at the mountains. "But I was thinking."

"What?"

"I was wondering if . . . well, I know this might sound lame, but maybe you'd kind of give me a painting lesson sometime? I was thinking it might be kind of cool."

"What would you want to paint?"

"I was thinking maybe *The View*. The way it was on Christmas."

"Well, I'm not all that great, but I guess I could give you a lesson. If you'll do something for me."

"What?"

"Teach me how to hit a curve ball?"

Picturing his klutzy brother at the plate, John

Henry couldn't help smirking. "Hitting a curve's not that easy, you know. You've got to have a really good eye."

"Oh, well, painting's a snap. And you don't need a good eye for that."

Tim said this so sarcastically that John Henry instinctively squared around, his hands fisting up inside his mittens, and for a moment the two boys stood facing off like prizefighters sizing each other up in the ring. But instead of slugging each other, they both just laughed, sending out puffs of vaporized breath that drifted into each other in the icy air.

WINIFRED V.
TUTTLE

1915-2000